Take Charge

Other fantastic books in the growing Faithgirlz™ library

BIBLES

The NIV Faithgirlz Bibles
The NKJV Faithgirlz Bible
NIV Faithgirlz Backpack Bibles

FICTION

Natalie Grant's Glimmer Girls Series

London Art Chase
(Book One)
A Dolphin Wish
(Book Two)
Miracle in Music City
(Book Three)
Light Up New York
(Book Four)

Samantha Sanderson Series

At the Movies (Book One)
On the Scene (Book Two)
Off the Record (Book Three)
Without a Trace (Book Four)

Good News Shoes Series

Riley Mae and the
Rock Shocker Trek
(Book One)
Riley Mae and the
Ready Eddy Rapids
(Book Two)
Riley Mae and the
Sole Fire Safari
(Book Three)

The Girls of Harbor View

Girl Power (Book One)
Take Charge (Book Two)
Raising Faith (Book Three)
Secret Admirer (Book Four)

Sophie's World Series (2 books in 1)

Meet Sophie
Sophie Steps Up
Sophie and Friends
Sophie's Friendship Fiasco
Sophie Flakes Out
Sophie's Drama

The Lucy Series

Lucy Doesn't Wear Pink
(Book One)
Lucy Out of Bounds
(Book Two)
Lucy's "Perfect" Summer
(Book Three)
Lucy Finds Her Way
(Book Four)

From Sadie's Sketchbook

Shades of Truth (Book One)
Flickering Hope (Book Two)
Waves of Light (Book Three)
Brilliant Hues (Book Four)

NONFICTION

Devotionals

No Boys Allowed
What's a Girl to Do?
Whatever Is Lovely
Shine on, Girl!
That Is So Me
Finding God in Tough Times
Girl Talk
Girlz Rock

Faithgirlz Bible Studies

The Secret Power of Love
The Secret Power of Joy
*The Secret Power of
Goodness*
The Secret Power of Grace

Lifestyle and Fun

Faithgirlz Journal
Faithgirlz Cookbook
True You
Best Party Book Ever!
101 Ways to Have Fun
*101 Things Every Girl
Should Know*
Best Hair Book Ever
Redo Your Room
God's Beautiful Daughter
*Everybody Tells Me
to Be Myself but I Don't Know
Who I Am*

Check out www.faithgirlz.com

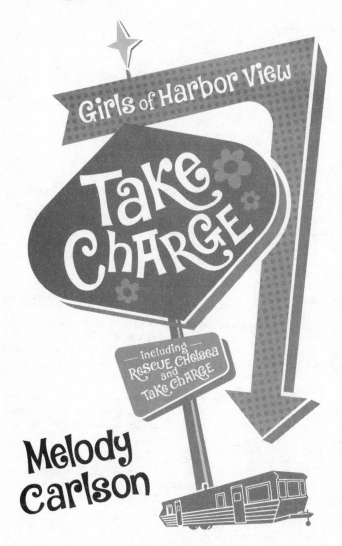

faithgirlz™

Girls of Harbor View

Take CHARGE

— including —
Rescue Chelsea
and
Take CHARGE

Melody
Carlson

ZONDERkidz

ZONDERKIDZ

Rescue Chelsea
Copyright © 2012 by Melody Carlson

Take Charge
Copyright © 2012 by Melody Carlson

This title is also available as a Zondervan ebook.
Visit www.zondervan.com/ebooks.

Requests for information should be addressed to:
Zonderkidz, 3900 Sparks Dr. SE, Grand Rapids, MI 49546

This edition: ISBN 978-0-310-75373-5

Library of Congress Cataloging-in-Publication Data

Carlson, Melody.
        [Project, take charge]
        Take charge / by Melody Carlson.
            p.   cm. — (Girls of Harbor View) (Faithgirlz!)
        Summary: When vandals trash McPhearson Park, Amy leads the way as she,
Morgan, Carlie, Emily, and Chelsea, the newest club member, make it their project
to save the spot from being turned into a parking lot and restore it to a place of
beauty and fun.
        ISBN 978-0-310-73046-0 (softcover)
        [1. Parks — Fiction. 2. Environmental protection — Fiction. 3. Friendship — Fiction.
4. Christian life — Fiction. 5. Oregon — Fiction.] I. Title.
        PZ7.C216637Tak 2012
        [Fic] — dc23   2011051692

Editor: Kim Childress
Cover design: Ron Huizinga

Printed in the United States

16 17 18 19 20 21 22 23 /DCI/ 19 18 17 16 15 14 13 12 11 10 9 8 7 6 5 4 3 2 1

So we fix our eyes not on what is seen, but what is unseen.
For what is seen is temporary, but what is unseen is eternal.

— 2 Corinthians 4:18

Rescue Chelsea

chapter one

"I can't hang with you guys today." Carlie kicked a rock with the toe of her sandal and frowned.

"Why not?" asked Morgan as she unlocked the door to the Rainbow Bus, the girls' clubhouse. "Did you forget that I was going to teach you how to do beads today?"

"No." Carlie rolled her eyes. "But Tia Maria is making me go to work with her today."

"Huh?" Emily peered curiously at Carlie. "Don't they have child labor laws in this state?"

"Yeah," said Amy. "First they make you babysit all the time and now they have you cleaning houses too? What's up with that?"

"I don't babysit *all the time*," Carlie corrected her. "Besides, I sometimes get paid for it when I do."

"Why do you have to go and help your aunt with housecleaning today?" asked Morgan.

"That's not what I'll be doing," Carlie explained. "I'm going with Tia Maria because she's working for this new family that moved to town last week. They have a girl who's the same grade as us, and she's all bummed about having to move here and not knowing anyone. And it doesn't help that school starts in a couple of weeks."

"So they're going to force you to become her friend?" questioned Amy. "Isn't that a little weird?"

Carlie nodded. "Yep. And that's exactly what I told Tia Maria too, but she won't take no for an answer. She's certain that I'm going to like this new girl."

"What if you don't?" asked Morgan.

Carlie shrugged. "Nothing I can do about that. But I got to thinking … I mean, I remember how it felt to be new in town last spring … and maybe I should try to make her feel welcome. Her name's Chelsea Landers. And, who knows, maybe she's nice."

"Well, if she is nice, maybe we should all get to know her," suggested Morgan. "Maybe she'll even want to join our club."

"I don't know," said Amy. "I mean, we've never talked about getting new members before. Do you guys really think it's a good idea?"

"I'm not so sure," admitted Emily. "The bus isn't really that big. With all four of us it can get kinda crowded."

"Well, there'll only be three of us today," Morgan pointed out. "Sorry you can't stay." Morgan smiled at Carlie. "But maybe I can show you how to do beads some other time."

"Yeah," said Carlie. "I hope so."

"Well, have fun," called Emily.

Carlie tried to hide her disappointment as she waved. "See ya guys later."

The other girls called out good-bye and Carlie slowly walked back toward her house. This really didn't seem fair. She'd already missed out on a lot of fun this summer because of babysitting her little brothers so much. Plus, she'd been looking forward to learning how to do beads for weeks now. But she had to be a "play date" for someone she didn't even know. She was tempted to tell Tia Maria to forget it, but Tia Maria was her favorite aunt and really cared about Carlie. So maybe she should just bite the bullet, put a smile on her face, and go.

"Hey, Carlie," called Tia Maria. She was standing by her little red car and waving. "I've been waiting for you."

"I'm coming," said Carlie. "I just had to tell my friends that I wouldn't be around today."

"I hope you don't mind too much," said Tia Maria.

Carlie shrugged as she got into the car. "It's okay. I mean, I do remember how lonely I felt when we first moved here."

"And then you made friends with the girls from the trailer court," Tia Maria reminded her. "And you've been happy as a clam ever since."

Carlie forced a smile. "Yeah, it's great having good friends." But she thought it would be even better if she actually got to hang with them sometimes!

"Especially when you're in middle school," Tia Maria pointed out. "I still remember how hard it was going to seventh grade. My best friend had moved away that summer and I felt like I didn't know a soul. I was so scared."

"Do you think that's how Chelsea feels?" asked Carlie. Tia Maria nodded. "Yeah. She's a gloomy girl."

Carlie sat up straighter now. "Well, I'll do my best to try and cheer her up. I just hope she's nice." The truth was, ever since moving to Boscoe Bay last spring, Carlie had been wishing for a best friend for herself. It seemed like Emily and Morgan had become best friends during the summer, and even though there was still Amy … well, Carlie just wasn't too sure. She and Amy were so completely different.

"Speaking of nice," said Tia Maria. "You look very pretty today."

Carlie frowned down at the flowery sundress. "Mom made me wear this. She wanted me to look like a lady." She groaned. "It's been so great getting to wear just shorts and T-shirts this summer. I was hoping that Mom would lighten up, you know, before school starts. But now I'm getting all worried again."

Tia Maria laughed. "My sister Lena can be a little old-fashioned."

"Tell me about it."

"Maybe I can talk to her for you, Carlie."

"Would you?" Carlie looked eagerly at her aunt. "She might actually listen to you!"

"Sure. I'd be happy too. It'll be my way of thanking you for coming with me today. Okay?"

"Sounds like a deal." Carlie leaned back. Maybe this day would be worth it. Even if Chelsea turned out to be a beast, at least Tia Maria might talk Mom into letting Carlie dress like a normal girl when school started up again this fall. It was hard enough being the new girl last spring, but having to dress like Little Miss Muffet made things way worse. She still remembered the time that Morgan suggested they walk home together — the day the bullies picked on them — and how Morgan had been surprised to discover that Carlie wasn't a sissy after all. And that was when things had really started to change.

"Chelsea's dad moved to Boscoe Bay to run the new bank," said Tia Maria as she turned into Pacific Shores and pushed some buttons to open a big iron gate. This was a fancy subdivision that Carlie had only seen from the road. "And their house is pretty nice."

"Wow," said Carlie as she looked out the window. "They all look pretty nice. I'll bet they cost a bundle too."

"Depends on whether or not you think half a million is a bundle."

"Half a million?" Carlie blinked. "These people must be rich."

Tia Maria laughed as she turned onto a street called Sunset Lane. "Or over their heads in debt."

"Are you and Mom still thinking of starting your own business?" asked Carlie. "I mean, now that you took that bookkeeping class?"

"There's a lot to do first," said Tia Maria as she pulled into the driveway of a beautiful house with pale yellow stucco walls. "But we're working on it."

"Good," said Carlie as she looked up at the house. "Maybe you guys will get so rich that we'll end up living in this neighborhood someday."

"Well, don't hold your breath," Tia Maria laughed. "But miracles can happen."

"Want some help?" asked Carlie as her aunt opened the tiny trunk of her car.

"No. This is a one-woman show." She lifted out a crate of cleaning supplies. "Besides, you don't want to get anything on your pretty dress."

Suddenly Carlie felt nervous. *What if this Chelsea chick is horrible? Or what if she doesn't like me? Or what if I do something totally lame? Something that embarrasses Tia Maria and makes her whole family look stupid. Oh, why did I agree to do this?*

"You coming?" asked her aunt as she walked over to a side door that went through the triple-car garage.

"Yeah," said Carlie, slowly following her.

"Don't worry," said Tia Maria as she held the door open for Carlie. "It'll be fine. Just relax."

Carlie took in a deep breath as she walked into the big, clean garage. "Wow, those are nice cars."

Tia Maria nodded then spoke in a hushed voice. "Money isn't everything, Carlie."

"I know."

"These are regular people ... just like us."

And the next thing Carlie knew they were in the house. Okay, it was only the laundry room, but it was the biggest, fanciest laundry room that Carlie had ever seen. The washer and dryer looked like they might be capable of flying to Mars or Venus.

"Hello?" called a woman's voice. "Is that you, Maria?"

"Yes." Tia Maria set her crate of cleaning supplies on a shiny countertop that looked like it was real stone. "And I've brought my niece with me."

"Oh, good." A tall, blonde woman came into the laundry room.

"This is Carlie Garcia," said Tia Maria. "And, Carlie, this is Mrs. Landers, Chelsea's mom."

They shook hands. "I'm so glad you could come, Carlie," said Mrs. Landers. "Poor Chelsea is really having a hard time adjusting to all this. She misses her old friends dearly."

"Well, I remember how hard it was when my family moved here last spring," said Carlie. "It's not easy making new friends."

"But Carlie's made some good ones," said Tia Maria.

"Well, come meet Chelsea," said Mrs. Landers. "Hopefully, you girls will become good friends too."

Carlie followed Mrs. Landers through the huge kitchen and family room. Carlie suspected it was as big as her whole house. Not only was it spacious, but everything in it looked brand-new and perfect — like something you'd see in a magazine. "Your house is really pretty," said Carlie.

"Thank you." Mrs. Landers smiled. "It's been a chore getting it all unpacked and set up. But it's slowly coming together. Your aunt has been a lifesaver."

Now they were going up a curving staircase that had a crystal chandelier suspended down the center of the open foyer. Carlie ran her hand along the polished wood banister and wondered if it would be good for sliding down on — not that she would do something like that. At least not if anyone was around to see her.

"Chelsea has a brother and a sister," explained Mrs. Landers. "But they're much older and don't live at home anymore. So I'm afraid she feels more lonely and isolated than ever."

"I can understand that."

Mrs. Landers paused by the closed door and knocked quietly. No one answered, and so she cracked open the door and called out, "Chelsea, I've got someone here who wants to meet you." Still no answer. She pushed the door fully open. "Chelsea?"

"Go away!" screamed a girl's voice. "Leave me alone! And take that freak with you!"

Carlie sucked in a quick breath. Maybe this wasn't such a good idea after all. Maybe Chelsea really was a monster. Oh, why had she ever agreed to come here today? What a total mistake!

chapter two

"Come on, Chelsea," urged Mrs. Landers as she slowly led Carlie into a large bedroom with a high ceiling. "You can't mope forever."

Carlie looked around the room. The walls and the carpet were pale blue, but the furnishings were all a creamy white. And the bedspread and pillows had touches of buttery yellow and shades of blue. Very pretty. But not too frilly. Still, it was nothing like any bedroom Carlie had ever seen before. Even her parents' master bedroom was way smaller than this. One wall was filled with built-in shelves that were loaded with every kind of entertainment option anyone could ever want, including a fairly large, flat-screen TV, a DVD player, and a computer. Several shelves were packed full with video games and DVDs. Carlie suppressed an unexpected wave of jealousy. This girl had everything!

Mrs. Landers walked across the room to where another door was half opened. It seemed to lead into a bathroom. Did Chelsea have her own private bathroom too? It was too much!

"I know you're not happy, sweetheart, but I just wanted you to —"

"Just leave me alone!" came the girl's voice from the bathroom again. She sounded even angrier now. "And take *her* with you!"

"Come out and meet Carlie," urged her mother as she went into the bathroom. "She's the same age as you and has only lived in Boscoe Bay a few months. I think you'll —"

"I don't want to meet anyone!"

Mrs. Landers came out of the bathroom helplessly holding her hands in the air, as if she was giving up.

"Maybe I should go," said Carlie.

"Oh, please, don't leave, not yet," pleaded Mrs. Landers. "Give Chelsea some time. I think she'll come around."

"The only way I'll ever come around will be to kill myself!" yelled the girl. "Not that anyone would care if I did!"

Mrs. Landers pointed over to the window and a big, padded window seat. "Why don't you just sit down and wait, Carlie? There are some magazines you can read."

Carlie wasn't so sure she wanted to stick around. The girl in the bathroom sounded horribly mean, not to mention slightly crazy. And yet, this poor woman seemed so desperate, how could Carlie just give up and leave?

"Okay," said Carlie, walking over to the cozy-looking window seat. "If you really think it'll help ... "

Mrs. Landers nodded then lowered her voice. "I think maybe if I wasn't here … maybe she would come out. You see, she's angry at us; she blames her dad and me for ruining her life."

"Oh." Carlie sat down on the window seat and looked out to see the ocean stretching out before her. "Wow, you guys have a great view from up here."

Mrs. Landers smiled sadly. "Yes, it's much prettier here than where we moved from. You'd think Chelsea would appreciate that."

"Chelsea would appreciate it if you would shut up!" yelled the girl from the bathroom.

Mrs. Landers made a little waving motion to Carlie then quickly left the room, closing the door behind her. *Great,* thought Carlie, *what if this girl is dangerous?* She glanced over to the still-opened bathroom door, unsure of what she should do next. Should she say something? Or maybe go in there … and risk getting her head chewed off? Maybe not.

Maybe she should just play it cool, just wait until Chelsea was ready to come out and have a civilized conversation. If that was even possible. Carlie picked up a glossy teen magazine and pretended to read it as she looked out the window to where the darker blue of the ocean met the lighter blue of the sky. It was such a gorgeous day outside. And here she was stuck with this spoiled brat who seemed to be intent on having a pity party for one. Suddenly Carlie really missed her friends back at the Rainbow Bus. But even more than that, she was so thankful that she had friends!

Out of sheer boredom, she actually started to read an article about skin care. She'd just gotten to the part about exfoliation — which was supposed to leave your skin looking *creamy and fresh* — when she heard Chelsea come out of the bathroom.

"Why are you still here?" asked Chelsea grumpily.

Carlie set the magazine aside. "Your mom told me to wait for you."

"Well, I'm telling you to leave."

Without answering, Carlie just looked at the girl. She was about Carlie's height with shoulder-length, curly red hair that looked like it hadn't been combed in days. Her freckled nose was slightly turned up and her eyes — probably her best feature — looked to be either green or blue. Carlie couldn't decide. She had on wrinkled, flannel pajama bottoms and a yellow tank top that looked like she'd slept in it for a week or so.

"You don't look very happy," said Carlie.

"Brilliant observation," snapped Chelsea.

"It's hard to move and leave friends behind … "

"Duh." But Chelsea took a few steps closer. It looked as if she was checking Carlie out now. "Why are you dressed like that?"

Carlie looked down at the sundress and frowned. "My mom. She makes me wear prissy-looking stuff like this. She wants me to act like a lady."

Chelsea laughed in a sarcastic way. "Well, you look like a total geek."

"Duh," said Carlie.

"I mean, that color and that style, well, it's like so yesterday."

Carlie shrugged. "I don't know about that. All I know is that I don't like it. I hate wearing dresses. If I had my way I'd burn them all."

"Parents are so lame." Chelsea sat down on the bed across from Carlie, still studying her with a slight scowl on her face. "And what's with your hair anyway?" she asked. "You trying to look like Salma Hayek or Penélope Cruz or something?"

Carlie blinked. "You really think I look like Salma or Penélope?"

"More like you're *trying* to look like them with all that hair. How can you stand all that long, curly stuff anyway?"

"You should talk," said Carlie, losing her temper now. "Look at that red mop top you're wearing — you look like a circus clown!"

Chelsea looked shocked, and Carlie felt really bad. Why did she say that? Then Chelsea stood up and walked over to a dresser with a big mirror on top and stared at herself.

"I'm sorry—"

"No … " said Chelsea slowly. "You're right. My hair does look like a clown's." She fluffed it up even more then turned around to show Carlie. "There, that's even better."

Carlie suppressed a giggle.

Chelsea looked down at her tank top and pajama bottoms. "I guess I don't really look like I should be handing out fashion advice, huh?"

"Not really." Carlie laughed nervously. "But you could pose for a *before* picture." She flipped the magazine open to show a section where girls had been made over by a panel of experts. "See, here's a *before* picture that looks a little like you."

"Thanks a lot."

"Sorry."

"Why did you come here anyway?" asked Chelsea as she sat back down on the bed again. "Do you live in the neighborhood or something?"

Carlie firmly shook her head. "No way. My aunt was doing some cleaning and stuff for your mom and she thought you seemed lonely."

"So they imported a little Mexican friend for me?"

"Yeah, whatever." Carlie looked out the window again. How she wished she was anywhere but here. She was tempted to act like Amy now, saying that she hadn't been born in Mexico and that she was an American — *thank you very much*! But she decided to just ignore her instead.

"Sorry," said Chelsea. "That wasn't very nice."

Carlie looked back at her. "You're right. It wasn't."

"I said I'm sorry."

Carlie just nodded. "Maybe I should go."

"No," said Chelsea, standing quickly as if to block Carlie from the door. "Look, I really am sorry. Sometimes I just say totally lame things like that. My shrink says I have no impulse control."

"Your shrink?"

"You know, my psychiatrist."

"You have a psychiatrist?"

"More like a counselor," said Chelsea. "And it's only been since we moved here. They all think I'm depressed."

"Are you?"

"Yeah, maybe so."

Carlie looked around her big room with all its cool stuff and sighed. "Man, if I lived here, I don't think I'd ever be depressed."

Chelsea rolled her eyes. "Haven't you ever heard that money can't buy love?"

"Who's trying to buy your love?"

"Who do you think? My parents. Duh."

"Oh."

"I suppose your parents don't do that."

Carlie laughed. "Not even. But they do pay me for babysitting. Of course, then they make me put half in savings and save the rest for school clothes."

"And then they pick out your school clothes?"

Carlie nodded. "Talk about a lose-lose situation."

"So are you poor then?"

Carlie pressed her lips together, determined not to say something she'd regret. Just because Chelsea had no impulse control, it didn't mean that Carlie should stoop to her level.

"Sorry," said Chelsea, looking believably contrite. "I guess I shouldn't have said that either."

So Carlie told Chelsea how they used to have a pretty nice house in Coswell. "My dad had a great job, and I had friends, and life seemed good. Then my dad got laid off and we had to move up here. It hasn't been real easy."

"Where do you live?"

"Harbor View."

"That sounds nice."

Carlie laughed. "Well, some parts of it are nice. I mean, I have three really good friends there. And we have this club where we hang out. But Harbor View is a trailer park."

"A trailer park?"

"Actually, it's a mobile-home park," said Carlie. "At least that's what my mom tells people. And we don't plan on living there forever. Just until we can save up some money for something better. And my mom and my aunt want to start a business."

"So what are your friends like?" asked Chelsea. "Are they poor too?"

Carlie gave Chelsea a warning look.

"Sorry." Chelsea slapped her hand over her mouth.

"It's just that saying things like that can hurt people's feelings," Carlie told her. "And besides we don't think of ourselves as poor. I mean, we have lots of fun and do all kinds of things, and you should see our clubhouse."

"You have a clubhouse?"

Carlie went into a detailed description of how they'd been given the bus by Mr. Greeley, the owner of the trailer park, and how they'd worked so hard to fix it up. She told about the kinds of things they liked to do together. "Like today," she said, "Morgan was going to teach us how to do beaded jewelry. Her mom has this cool shop down on the waterfront. It's called Cleo's, and she has beads and all kinds of imported stuff. And Morgan is really creative. She can make almost anything. We think she'll be a real designer someday."

"She sounds pretty cool," said Chelsea. "I know you wouldn't guess it by looking at me today, but I'm usually into fashion too."

Then Carlie told her about Amy and Emily. "We're all really different," she finally said, "but it's like we go together."

"I think I'd like to meet your friends."

Carlie nodded, but she had some concerns about this. She wasn't sure that a girl like Chelsea would really get them. She might even make fun of her friends or their bus. That would definitely not be good. She decided to change the subject. "Can you get to the beach from your house?"

"I guess."

"You guess?" Carlie frowned at this strange girl. "You mean you haven't even been down there yet?"

Chelsea shrugged. "I didn't want to."

"Well, do you want to now?"

Chelsea brightened a little. "I guess so."

Carlie pointed to her pajama bottoms. "So you really wanna wear your little yellow rubber ducky pajamas on the beach? I mean, we might see someone, you never know."

Chelsea smiled. "Maybe not." Then she looked at Carlie. "You really wanna wear that goofy looking dress on the beach?"

Carlie sighed. "Guess I don't have much choice."

"We're about the same size," said Chelsea. "Why don't you borrow something?" Then she opened a door and flicked on a light, and there was the biggest closet Carlie had ever seen.

"Sheesh," said Carlie. "Your closet is bigger than my bedroom."

Chelsea just shrugged. "Go ahead and find something you want to wear. I think maybe I should take a shower."

Carlie nodded. "Yeah, I think that'd be a good idea."

Chelsea made a face. "I smell that bad, huh?"

"Well, no offense, but I'm guessing your personal hygiene's been a little neglected lately."

Chelsea laughed. "That's putting it mildly."

So while Chelsea showered, Carlie picked out a pair of denim shorts and an orange tank top and slipped them on. So much better! Before long, Chelsea was showered and dressed and the two of them headed downstairs.

"We're going to the beach, Mom," called Chelsea as they trekked through the kitchen where Mrs. Landers was unloading a box of fancy goblets. She just blinked and nodded; and then when Chelsea wasn't looking, she gave Carlie a quick thumbs-up.

"I think the trail to the beach is a couple of houses down," said Chelsea. "I saw the sign when we were moving in."

Sure enough, there was the trail, leading to some steps that took them right down to the beach.

"What a glorious day!" said Carlie, lifting her arms as she turned in a happy circle. "It's crazy to stay cooped up on a day like this." Then she kicked off her sandals and ran straight toward the surf, screaming with delight when the cold water washed up around her feet. Chelsea stood back, a little unsure, but then she kicked off her flip-flops and joined her. Soon they were daring each other to go out farther and farther, and before long they were both dog-paddling through the waves.

"That water is freezing cold," said Chelsea when they finally got out.

"Yep," said Carlie. "Doesn't it make you feel alive?"

"Makes me feel like I wish I'd brought a towel."

"The sun will warm us," said Carlie as she picked up her sandals. "Let's just walk on the beach for a while until we're dry."

"Okay," said Chelsea. "If you're sure we won't catch pneumonia and die out here first."

Carlie laughed. "For a girl who was threatening to kill herself just an hour ago, I'm surprised that you'd be the least bit worried about pneumonia now."

"Yeah, whatever!" As they walked, Chelsea opened up a little. And Carlie began to relax some. Maybe this wasn't such a mistake after all.

chapter three

As they walked down the beach, Chelsea told Carlie about her best friend that she'd left behind when they moved here. "I mean, Audrey and I had been very best friends ever since second grade," she said. "She was like the only person on the entire planet who totally got me."

"But you can still be friends," said Carlie. "You can write or phone or email her. There are lots of ways to stay in touch."

"She already made a new best friend," said Chelsea in a hurt voice, "with this other girl named Kirsten Powers, and she's such a jerk. She just couldn't wait for me to leave. I mean, seriously, the second I was gone, Kirsten jumped in and took my place with Audrey." She sighed. "Now they do everything together. I don't think Audrey even misses me at all."

"Oh, I bet she does."

"Ha!" Chelsea bent down to pick up a stone and tossed it out into the ocean.

"Well, if that's true," said Carlie. "Then maybe it's time you start making some new friends anyway."

"Yeah. I'm sure that's easier said than done."

"It's a whole lot easier when you're not a total grump."

"Are you saying I'm a total grump?" asked Chelsea.

"Hey, that's putting it mildly. You were way worse than a grump when I met you earlier today."

"Thanks a lot." She made a pouting face then put her hands on her messy hair. "Can I help it if I was having a bad hair day?"

Carlie laughed.

"You're hair is almost as curly as mine, Carlie. I'd think you would understand."

She nodded. "Yeah, I guess I kinda do."

"So I haven't scared you off for good yet?"

"I guess I'm getting used to you."

"And I guess I'm getting hungry," said Chelsea suddenly. "I wonder what time it is anyway?"

So they turned around and headed back. And by the time they were in Chelsea's kitchen again, Carlie was actually starting to feel comfortable around this strange girl. She was even starting to get used to their very fancy house. She didn't see her aunt anywhere, but she figured she was probably busy cleaning something or putting something away. It was still kind of strange to think that Tia Maria was here to work and Carlie was here to play, but there wasn't much she could do about it anyway.

"Is there anything to eat around here?" Chelsea asked her mom.

"There's some leftover pasta and salad," said her mom.

"I mean something *good.*"

Her mom just smiled. "Well, what sounds good to you girls?"

"Pizza!" said Chelsea. "Double cheese and pepperoni."

"How about if I have one delivered?" said her mom happily.

"Sounds good."

Mrs. Landers reached over and touched Chelsea's still damp hair. "Did you girls go swimming? I didn't see you out by the pool."

"We went swimming in the ocean," Chelsea proudly told her.

Mrs. Landers looked surprised. "You swam in the ocean? That's, uh, very interesting."

"And it was really cold."

Her mom nodded. "I'll phone in the pizza. Why don't you go get cleaned up."

"You have a pool?" asked Carlie as they walked toward the stairs.

"Yeah." Chelsea pointed toward the glass windows in the family room. But the shades were pulled and Carlie couldn't see outside. "It's out there."

"Cool," said Carlie.

Chelsea looked slightly surprised. "Don't tell me you want to go swimming again?"

"Sure!" said Carlie. "Why not?"

So for the rest of the afternoon, Carlie and Chelsea swam in the pool, ate pizza, drank pop, sunned themselves, and just had plain old fun. When they got too hot outside, they went up to Chelsea's room and started playing video games. Chelsea beat Carlie at most of them. Still, Carlie didn't mind. She was just glad to see Chelsea happy and acting like a normal girl.

"What's up with the bracelet?" asked Chelsea, pointing to the special bracelet that Morgan had made for her friends. "What do the letters mean? LYNAY? Is that like your middle name or something?"

"It's an acronym," said Carlie as she adjusted the bracelet. "It has to do with our club."

"So what do the letters stand for?"

Carlie wondered if someone like Chelsea would even get it. Not that it mattered since it was supposed to be a secret anyway. "We're not supposed to tell. It's for club members only."

Chelsea rolled her eyes. "You and your dumb club."

"It's not dumb."

"Well, why do you have secrets?"

"All clubs have secrets. It just makes it more fun."

Chelsea looked at the letters. "Let's see ... I think it stands for Last ... Year's ... Nerds ... Are ... Yutzes."

"Real nice."

"That's it! Last year's nerds are yutzes. I've solved the mystery!" Chelsea laughed loudly.

Despite trying to appear offended, Carlie started laughing with her. "Well, that should include you too, Chelsea. Last year's nerds are yutzes. What are yutzes anyway?"

"I don't know. It just sounds like it fits."

"I hate to interrupt the party," said Tia Maria as she tapped on the door, "but it's time to go now."

"This was fun," Carlie told Chelsea as she stood up.

"Yeah, I'm glad you came over," said Chelsea as she followed them downstairs. "Even if I *didn't* invite you."

Carlie wasn't sure how to respond to that.

"But I would've invited you," said Chelsea quickly. "If I'd known you, that is."

"Well, thanks for everything." To Carlie's surprise, she was almost sad to leave. It almost felt like she'd spent a day in paradise, actually living out the "lifestyles of the rich and famous." She was afraid she could get used to this.

"Can you come back again tomorrow?" asked Chelsea eagerly.

Carlie could see Chelsea's mom standing behind her daughter vigorously nodding her head.

"I'm not sure," admitted Carlie. "But I can ask my mom and call you later."

So the girls exchanged phone numbers, and Carlie and Tia Maria got in the little red car and started driving across town.

"Sounds like you two hit it off pretty well," said her aunt.

"Yeah, I guess so."

"I know that Mrs. Landers was hugely relieved to see Chelsea coming out of her slump."

"Yeah, Chelsea was acting pretty weird when I first got there. I can see why her mom was worried."

"Well, I owe you one, Carlie. And if you still want me to talk to your mom about school clothes, I'll be glad to!"

"Cool!"

"So are you going to introduce Chelsea to your other friends?"

Carlie considered this. "I don't know … maybe not right away. I guess I should get to know her better first."

Earlier today, Carlie had felt worried that Chelsea might offend her friends by saying something rude or mean. But now she wasn't so sure she wanted her friends to get to know Chelsea for a totally different reason. Carlie knew that Morgan, Emily, and Amy were pretty cool and interesting girls — maybe even more interesting than Carlie. What if Chelsea liked one of her friends better than she liked Carlie? As selfish as that sounded, Carlie wasn't sure she could handle it.

"I'm going in to chat with my sister," said Tia Maria as she pulled into Carlie's driveway.

"Cool," said Carlie, getting out of the car.

"Hey, Carlie!" called Morgan from the other side of the street.

"Hey!" Carlie yelled back as she headed over to where her three friends were waving at her. "I'm so glad to see you guys!"

"How'd it go today?" asked Amy.

"And what do you think of the new girl?" asked Morgan.

"She's pretty nice," said Carlie. Then she laughed. "Well, to be honest, she was kinda scary to start with. But then we talked and stuff. And I think she's okay."

"Do you think she'll want to join our club?" asked Morgan.

Carlie considered this. "Maybe. But I think I should get to know her better first."

"And we still need to decide whether or not we're open to new members," said Amy. "We need to discuss it and vote on it."

"I vote yes," said Emily.

"This isn't an official meeting," said Amy.

"We do need to talk it through before we start voting." Then Morgan carefully removed something from her shorts pocket. "We made this for you, Carlie." She held up a choker of red and purple beads.

"Oh, that's beautiful!" exclaimed Carlie. "Really, you made this for me?"

"We all helped," said Amy.

"Thanks," said Carlie as Emily helped her to fasten it in back. She smiled at her friends. "You guys are so great. I'm so lucky to have you!"

"I have to go," said Amy as she glanced at her watch. "I'm supposed to help at the restaurant tonight."

"I better go inside too," said Carlie. "I'm sure my mom is wondering why I didn't come in. See ya later!"

Carlie fingered the beaded necklace as she went into her house. Her friends were the best! Even if Chelsea did live in a big, fancy house with a swimming pool. Carlie would rather have friends like Morgan, Emily, and Amy any day!

chapter four

Carlie entered her house through the front door just in time to overhear Tia Maria's and her mom's loud voices coming from the kitchen. It sounded like they were having an argument. In Spanish. It was funny how her mom seemed to assume that if they argued in Spanish, Carlie and her little brothers wouldn't understand what they were saying. But Carlie knew enough Spanish to eavesdrop, and it only took a few seconds before she figured out that this hot-headed disagreement was about her.

"Why are you so stubborn?" Tia Maria's voice got louder.

"She's my only daughter!" said Carlie's mom. "I want her to dress like a girl! You go and have your own daughter and then you can dress her how you like."

"But it makes her look different," argued Tia Maria.

"Carlotta *is* different," said Mom. "She's my pretty little girl!"

"She's going to seventh grade soon. Do you want kids to pick on her because she's dressed like *your pretty little girl?*"

"Why should they pick on her for that?"

"She's not a baby anymore, Lena!"

Now Carlie came fully into the room. And Tia Maria just held up her hands and shook her head. "Sorry, *mija*," she said to Carlie. "I'm not getting through to my big, smart sister."

Mom looked at Carlie. "You don't want to look pretty?"

Carlie felt bad, but she wanted to be honest. "I just want to dress like other kids. I don't want to stick out … like *there goes that weird Latina girl*."

"Is that what your friends think?"

"Maybe my friends don't. But other kids do, Mom. Besides, I've been saving my babysitting money all summer long, and I just want to use it to buy some normal things, like some nice jeans and T-shirts — the kinds of stuff that other girls wear to school."

"But that's not ladylike, Carlotta," insisted Mom.

"Listen, Lena," said Tia Maria in a calming voice. "Carlie always acts like a lady, whether she's wearing a frilly dress or old blue jeans. Why can't you let her dress in a way that makes her feel good about herself?"

Mom frowned. "I don't know … "

"Please, Mom," Carlie pleaded.

Mom sighed loudly. "I'll talk to your father about this, Carlotta."

Carlie looked at Tia Maria in time to see her wink. They both knew this would settle everything. Dad would side with Carlie.

"Thanks, Mom," said Carlie, giving her mom a big hug. "I'll watch the boys while you make dinner."

"See," said Tia Maria. "She's a good girl, Lena. You should be proud."

Mom said a word in Spanish that Carlie didn't understand, but she had a strong feeling she shouldn't ask either. Instead she gathered up her little brothers and took them outside to play in the backyard for a while. It was actually Carlie's special place — her secret garden — but she and Dad had fixed up part of it as a play area for the boys. She opened the lid to the sandbox, and both boys dove for the dump truck. She turned on the hose and began watering some of her flowers, listening as her brothers argued over whose turn it was to use the shovel now.

"Hey, Carlie," called Tia Maria as she came outside a few minutes later. "Mrs. Landers just called me on my cell phone, and she's begging me to bring you again tomorrow. Chelsea is going to call and invite you tonight. But please consider it, mija. Mrs. Landers thinks that you made a good connection with Chelsea and she was so happy about it. Chelsea really likes you."

"Oh … " Carlie lifted up Pedro, who was crying because Miguel had thrown a handful of sand in his face. She held him on her hip as she brushed sand from his mouth and scolded Miguel. Carlie considered the invitation to the Landers' and wondered how she could turn it down without hurting anyone. She'd really been hoping to hang with her old friends tomorrow.

"Not that you owe me anything … " Her aunt gave her a sly grin now. "But it does look like you're going to get to wear what you like to school this year. That is worth a little something, isn't it?"

Carlie had to smile. "Yeah, that was good. Thanks."

"So will you go with me again tomorrow?"

"Okay," she agreed. How could she not?

"Thanks!"

The next morning, Carlie decided to give her mom a little test. What would happen if she wore her favorite khaki shorts and a T-shirt to Chelsea's house today? Would Mom make her go back to her room and change into something more "ladylike"?

"That's not what you're wearing to visit your new friend, is it, Carlotta?" Mom asked as she filled a bowl with Cheerios.

"Yeah." Carlie avoided eye contact as she slipped into a kitchen chair.

"Maria says this Landers family is very wealthy," said Mom as she helped Pedro into his booster seat. "She says they're influential. Mr. Landers is president of the new bank. Don't you want to make a good impression?"

"It's okay, Mom. In fact, yesterday Chelsea thought I looked kinda weird because I had on a dress. She even mentioned it. I'm just trying to dress the way she does. I think it makes her more comfortable."

"Oh." Mom seemed to consider this as she poured milk on Pedro's cereal.

Carlie hurried to finish her breakfast before Mom had a chance to come up with another reason why she should go and change her clothes. Then, to her relief, Tia Maria arrived. Carlie grabbed up her backpack with her swimsuit and other things in it and told her mom good-bye.

"Your mom is easing up on the dress code already?" her aunt asked as she got into the car.

"Yeah." Carlie smiled. "With a little more than two weeks until school starts, I figure I might as well get her used to this."

"But promise me something, Carlie," said her aunt. "Promise me you won't start wearing sleazy-looking clothes like I see on some teenage girls. You won't go around with your belly or your hind end hanging out, will you?"

Carlie laughed. "No way! That's gross."

"Good. Because Lena would kill me if that happened."

"Don't worry," Carlie assured her. "I'm not like that. Not at all."

Her aunt seemed to relax. "Yes. I'm sure you're not."

"So can I ask you another favor, Tia Maria?"

"What is it?"

"Well, do you think you could try to talk to Mom about something else for me?"

Tia Maria groaned. "Oh, dear! Not another knock-down, drag-out fight with my sister!"

"Hopefully not."

"Well, if it has to do with piercing any body parts or tattoos or coloring your hair, just forget about it, little girl."

Carlie laughed. "No. But it does have to do with my hair. I want to cut it."

Her aunt frowned. "You know how your mother loves your hair long, Carlie."

"I know, but it's my hair. And I get so tired of it. And it's so hot and it's always getting tangled. Even if I could just cut it to my shoulders, like Chelsea's. That would be way better."

"Hey, that gives me an idea," said her aunt. "Let me get back to you on the haircut business, okay?"

"No problem!"

Chelsea came out to meet Carlie in the driveway. "Hey, you didn't wear a party dress again today."

Carlie laughed. "Yeah, we're working on my mom."

"So what are we going to do today?" Chelsea asked eagerly.

"I don't know … what do you want to do?"

"Well, I haven't really been into town much." She rolled her eyes. "Not that there's much to see; it's a pretty small town. But I was thinking maybe I should check it out, you know?"

Carlie nodded. "That's a good idea."

"My mom said she'll take us if we want to go."

Carlie eyed the two fancy cars in the garage. "Can we ride in the white convertible?" she asked.

"Yeah, whatever."

"With the top down?"

Chelsea laughed. "Sure, if you want."

So Mrs. Landers drove the two girls to town in the Mercedes with the top down. Carlie felt like she was starring in a movie.

"Just call me when you want to be picked up," Mrs. Landers told them as she dropped them in the center of town. "You have your cell phone with you, don't you, Chelsea?"

Chelsea patted her purse. "Got it, Mom."

"And remember, your dad is right over there at the bank," Mrs. Landers said, pointing to the tall building across the street. "If you have an emergency or need something ... "

"Yeah, yeah ... "

"Have fun, girls!" Then Chelsea's mom drove away.

"Where to first?" asked Chelsea.

"We could go down to the waterfront," suggested Carlie. "It's only three blocks that way and there are some cool stores down there."

So they spent a couple of hours checking out the waterfront shops, including Cleo's where Carlie introduced

Chelsea to Morgan's mom.

"So your friend Morgan is black?" Chelsea asked after they left the shop.

"Huh?" Carlie wasn't sure if she'd heard her right.

"Morgan is African-American?" said Chelsea.

Carlie nodded. "Yeah, sure."

"I never had a friend who was black before," said Chelsea.

"Why not?"

"The school I went to had black kids in it, but they kept to themselves. And the white kids did too. I mean, it's like we didn't have anything in common with them anyway. So why bother getting to know them?"

"Well, I'm sure you'll like Morgan. She's very cool. Not only that, she's so much fun. She has all these ideas … she's totally creative."

"Her mom seemed okay … I mean for a black lady."

Carlie wondered what that was supposed to mean but didn't want to ask. Instead she just got quiet as they walked past a candle shop.

"I mean, it's not that I'm prejudiced," said Chelsea quickly. "It's just kind of weird, you know? I'm not used to it. Do kids at your school give you a bad time for having a black friend?"

Carlie considered this. "Some kids will give you a bad time for almost anything. And in case you haven't noticed,

I'm not exactly white."

"But that's different."

"How?" asked Carlie, feeling irritated now.

"I don't know … it just is."

"So, have you ever had a Hispanic friend before?" asked Carlie, unsure if she really wanted to know the answer to this either.

"Nope."

"But you're okay with it?"

"Sure. I like you."

"I like you too, Chelsea. But you gotta admit we're different." Carlie wanted to point out that Chelsea was rich.

"I'm hungry," said Chelsea as they walked past the Waterfront Cinema.

"Me too," said Carlie. "There's a McDonald's a couple of blocks up there near the wharf."

"McDonald's is so cheesy."

"Well, you don't *have* to get a *cheese*burger."

Chelsea laughed. "See, that's what I like about you, Carlie. You have a wacky sense of humor."

Carlie also had less money to waste on lunch, and McDonald's was good enough for her. She'd stuck a few bucks in her pocket this morning. She hadn't even been sure why, maybe it was *just in case*. But she knew she didn't have enough for anything beyond cheap, fast food.

"My mom gave us money to have lunch in town," said Chelsea as they paused on a corner. "Do you know of a good restaurant? I mean, besides McDonald's?"

Carlie thought for a few seconds. Her family didn't eat out much. "My friend Amy has a restaurant in town. I mean, her parents do. I've only been there once. It's pretty nice though."

"Why don't we go there?"

So they walked back to the business section of town and Carlie pointed out Asian Garden from across the street.

"A Chinese restaurant?" said Chelsea with surprise.

"You don't like Chinese food?"

"No, I like it okay."

"Actually, they have more than just Chinese food. They have Thai and a couple of other kinds too. I can't remember what though."

"Is your friend Chinese?"

"Amy?"

"Yeah, the one whose family owns the restaurant."

"They're Vietnamese," said Carlie. "But Amy was born in America, and she makes a big point of letting everyone know that she's American."

"Wow," said Chelsea. "You have a black friend and a Chinese —"

"Not Chinese," Carlie corrected, "*Vietnamese.*"

"Yeah, right. That's what I meant. But don't you think that's just a little bit weird?"

"Why?"

"I mean you're Mexican and—"

"I'm not really Mexican," said Carlie. "I mean my family hasn't lived in Mexico for several generations. So we're Americans too. But we are Hispanic or Latino."

"I didn't mean to offend you." Chelsea frowned as if Carlie was the one with the problem. "So do you want to eat there or not?"

"You decide." Carlie was seriously irritated at her new friend now. She realized she didn't really know Chelsea very well. And if Chelsea was having a problem with Carlie's friends before she'd even met them … well, that didn't seem like a very good sign. Right now all Carlie wanted was to be back at the Rainbow Bus with good friends who understood and accepted each other for who and what they were.

chapter five

Chelsea decided she wanted to eat at Asian Garden, but now Carlie wasn't so sure. Hopefully Chelsea wouldn't say anything to offend someone in Amy's family. Amy's sister Ly was working as hostess today. "Hi, Carlie," she said cheerfully as the girls went inside. "How are you doing?"

"Good," said Carlie. "This is my friend Chelsea. She just moved to town a couple of weeks ago."

Ly smiled. "Nice to meet you, Chelsea. Are you girls here for lunch?"

Carlie nodded. "Yeah. I've been showing Chelsea around town, and we got hungry."

"You came to the right place. This way," she said as she led them to a small table next to the bubbling fountain.

"They have real fish in there," said Carlie, pointing down to where a giant goldfish was swimming by.

"Cool," said Chelsea as they sat down.

Ly handed them menus. "Enjoy your meal."

"Thanks," said Chelsea.

"That's Amy's oldest sister," said Carlie as Ly walked away.

"She's pretty."

"Yeah," said Carlie, relieved to hear something positive for a change. "Amy has two older sisters and one older brother. They're way older though, like in their twenties, and I think Amy said Ly might be close to thirty, although I think she looks pretty young for her age."

"That's kind of like my family," said Chelsea. "My brother's twenty-three and my sister's twenty-one. I've heard my mom tell her friends that I was an unexpected surprise."

Carlie nodded. "Amy said that's how it was with her too. And I think her parents are even older than yours."

"I'm sorry if I sounded rude when we were outside," said Chelsea. "I mean, when I was asking about your friends and everything. I'm sure it came out all wrong. But it's just kinda weird, you know. Like I'm wondering does everyone have to be from a different race to join your club?"

Carlie giggled. "Well, we haven't really made rules yet. But I'm certain that wouldn't be one of them."

"So are white girls allowed then?"

"Of course. Emily is a white girl."

"How many girls are in your club anyway?"

"Just four. But we only started it in June. And our clubhouse — the bus, you know — isn't very big so I doubt that we'll ever have too many members."

"Oh ... "

Carlie wasn't sure what to say now. Was Chelsea trying to hint that she'd like to be invited to join their club? But after all the other comments about Carlie's friends, girls Chelsea hadn't even met … well, it didn't seem like such a good idea. Not yet anyway.

"Would you like tea?" asked Amy's other sister An.

"Yes, please," said Carlie. "Do you remember me, An? I'm Amy's friend from — "

"Oh, yes," said An with a smile. "I do remember you now. You're Carlie. I didn't recognize you at first."

So Carlie introduced Chelsea to her as well.

"Amy is supposed to come in to help out this afternoon," said An as she filled their water glasses. "But not until three. You'll probably be finished and gone by then."

"Too bad," said Chelsea. "I'd like to meet her."

"Do you live in Harbor View too?" asked An.

"No, I live in Pacific Shores."

An's eyebrows lifted up. "I've heard that's very nice."

"Yes," said Carlie. "It is."

"Does the whole family work here?" asked Chelsea after An left.

"Yeah," said Carlie. "I think so."

"That must be weird."

"I don't know," said Carlie. "My dad works with my uncle. And my mom and my aunt want to go into business together. I think it'd be fun to work with my own family."

Chelsea shook her head. "No way. I cannot imagine having to work at my dad's bank."

Carlie laughed. "Well, you're not old enough to anyway."

Both girls seemed to relax as they ate their lunch, and by the time they finished, Carlie thought maybe her earlier worries about Chelsea were silly. Sure, Chelsea seemed to just say whatever popped into her head, and sometimes that was offensive, but Carlie had to admit she was fun too.

"What's your fortune say?" asked Chelsea.

Carlie uncurled the slip of paper. "Beware of handsome strangers bearing beautiful gifts."

"Ooh," said Chelsea, "that's kinda creepy. We better be careful in town today. Maybe someone is going to try and kidnap you."

"Yuck." Carlie made a face. "I don't think so. What's yours say?"

"Your sunny disposition will draw many friends to you." She laughed. "Ya think?"

Carlie chuckled. "Well, you weren't exactly sunny yesterday."

"But you didn't give up on me, Carlie." Chelsea smiled. "We're friends, aren't we?"

"Sure."

Chelsea paid their bill, and they went back outside. "This town is pretty small potatoes," said Chelsea, looking up and down Main Street. "Where do you go to buy clothes?"

Carlie shrugged. "I've only lived here a few months."

"So where are you going to shop for school clothes?"

"I don't know."

"Well, it's only a couple of weeks until school starts. Don't you think you should find out?"

"I guess."

"I know," said Chelsea. "I'll ask my mom to take us to Portland. I think they've got some big malls there."

"Cool," said Carlie.

"But what should we do now?" asked Chelsea. "It seems like we've seen everything that's worth seeing around here."

"And it's sure getting hot," said Carlie, squinting in the bright afternoon sun. "Do you want to call your mom?"

So Chelsea called her mom, and the girls went over to the city park to wait in the shade for her. Sitting in the swings, they talked about what they thought it would be like to go to seventh grade.

"I'm kinda scared," admitted Chelsea.

"Why?"

"What if no one likes me?"

"I like you," said Carlie.

"But you might not like me as well as you like your other friends."

Carlie wasn't sure how to respond to that. It was probably true. Carlie did feel more comfortable with her other friends. Yet something about Chelsea was interesting too. She was different from anyone else that Carlie had known before.

"Promise that you'll be my friend when school starts," said Chelsea suddenly.

"Sure," said Carlie. "Why wouldn't I be?"

"I don't know ..."

"Don't worry," Carlie assured her. "I'll be your friend, and I'm sure my friends will too."

"I hope so." Chelsea pointed out to the street. "There's my mom."

The two girls hung out by Chelsea's pool again, and when they got too hot, they went inside and watched a DVD.

"Time to go, mija," said Tia Maria as she poked her head into Chelsea's bedroom.

"What's *mija* mean?" asked Chelsea as she turned off the TV.

"It's kind of like *my dear girl*," said Carlie's aunt.

"Thanks for everything," called Carlie as she shoved her damp swimsuit into her backpack.

"I'll call you," said Chelsea.

As Tia Maria drove toward home, Carlie asked her how long she would be working at the Landers.

"After they're all settled and unpacked and everything, I'll only clean once a week."

"They seem pretty settled now."

"There's still a lot to do," said her aunt. "There are boxes of books, and the pantry needs to be organized ... I'll probably be there for the rest of the week." She glanced at Carlie. "Why?"

"I was just curious."

"Does it make you feel weird that your aunt is cleaning house for your friend?"

Carlie laughed. "No, not at all."

"Good. You and Chelsea seem to have really hit it off. Mrs. Landers is so relieved that Chelsea's not moping around anymore. In fact, that reminds me of something ... something I promised you."

"What?"

"I spoke to Mrs. Landers about haircuts. I asked her who cuts her hair. And Chelsea's."

"*And?*"

"And she said she needed to find someone. And she said that Chelsea wanted to get hers cut before school starts."

"*And?*"

"And she said maybe you and Chelsea could get your hair cut together, and that she'd be happy to find a good place and take you both in."

"Oh, that'd be so cool!"

"So I'm thinking … if I present it like that to your mom … well, maybe she'll actually consider it."

Carlie crossed her fingers. "I hope so!"

This time Carlie took her little brothers out to play while Tia Maria went inside to talk to her sister. "We'll be down at the beach," she told Mom.

"Be careful," called her mom. "Keep a close eye on Pedro."

"Of course, I will."

Carlie ran into Morgan and Emily as she was heading down the trail to the beach.

"Howdy, stranger," said Morgan. "Where you been?"

"I had to go see Chelsea again today." Carlie grabbed Miguel's hand to stop him from going on down the trail without her.

"You *had* to?" questioned Emily.

"Well, my aunt did me a favor, so I sort of had to do that for her."

"You going to the beach now?" asked Morgan.

"These guys need some exercise."

"Want us to come along?" offered Emily as she swooped up little Pedro and tickled his tummy until he giggled.

"Sure!" Carlie smiled. "I've missed you guys so much."

So the three girls herded the two little boys down to the beach.

"So was Chelsea less grumpy today?" asked Morgan as they all waded in the water.

"Yeah," said Carlie. "We went to town and walked around. And we even went to your mom's shop and then to Amy's restaurant for lunch."

"When are you going to invite her here?" asked Emily.

"I don't know, " Carlie said.

"Don't we get to meet her?" asked Morgan.

"Of course," said Carlie. "I'm just not sure when."

"Well, Amy and Emily and I were discussing our membership rules this morning," said Morgan. "Not officially … but just talking about it, you know. And we've decided that if you like Chelsea enough to invite her over here, we'll be happy to consider her for membership."

"That's nice," said Carlie. But even as she said this, she wondered if it would really work. What would happen if Chelsea said something offensive to one of her friends? Or what if they just didn't like her? Even worse, Carlie wondered, how would she feel if Chelsea didn't like them?

"There's no rush," said Morgan. "You might want to get to know her better."

"Yeah," said Carlie. "I think that's a good idea."

"But you could always ask her over here just to hang out," said Emily. "Just so we could get to know her too."

Carlie nodded. "Okay. I'll mention that to her."

"Are you going back over there again tomorrow?" asked Morgan.

"I don't know," admitted Carlie. "I'm kinda hoping that I'll get to hang with you guys tomorrow. It seems like it's been a long time."

Morgan grinned. "Yeah, we were starting to get worried. We thought maybe you were leaving us in the dust. Like we might have to find someone to replace you in the club."

"Not that we would," said Emily quickly.

"Thanks," said Carlie. "And, don't worry. I would way rather be here with you guys than with Chelsea. But I know she's kinda lonely and she's scared about starting a new school with no friends."

"That's an even better reason to invite her over here," pointed out Morgan.

Carlie nodded. "You're right."

The girls chased Pedro and Miguel around until Carlie realized it would soon be suppertime at her house. "We better get back," she told her friends. "But thanks for helping me with the boys."

Of course, the boys protested when Carlie said it was time to go home. It took all three girls to herd the reluctant boys back to the trailer park again. Carlie wondered how her mom managed these boys day after day, especially during the summer when Dad worked such long hours on the fishing boat. She also wondered how her mom would do it without Carlie around to help.

chapter six

Carlie yelled thanks to Emily and Morgan as she dragged her two little brothers into the house. She noticed that Tia Maria's car was gone and was curious how the haircutting conversation had gone, but she got so distracted trying to get her brothers cleaned up for supper that she forgot to ask her mom. It wasn't until she was helping to clear the table that she remembered Tia Maria's promise to talk to her. Even so, Carlie wasn't so sure she wanted to ask. Mom seemed stressed as she cleaned up Miguel's spilled glass of milk on the floor — the second one tonight. Carlie decided it might be better to keep quiet and finish cleaning up the kitchen first.

"Phone, Carlotta," called Mom as Carlie placed the last plate in the dishwasher.

Carlie picked it up in the kitchen. "Hello?"

"Hi, Carlie," said Chelsea in a happy voice. "Guess what?"

"Aliens have landed and they've invited you to go away with them?"

"No, silly. My mom wants to take us both to get our hair cut on Saturday."

"Really?" Now Carlie wasn't sure what to say. She didn't even know if her mom would let her cut her hair. This could turn embarrassing.

"Yeah," continued Chelsea. "She already made us appointments at this really cool place that her friend told her about. It's in Portland. Her friend Leslie lives there, and we can spend the night at her house. And we'll have time to go shopping too!"

"Wow, that sounds awesome," said Carlie. "But I'll have to check with my mom first."

"Call me back as soon as you know," said Chelsea.

So Carlie hung up. She turned on the dishwasher and finished wiping down all the countertops in the kitchen. She was trying to think of a good way to ask Mom something this big. And, okay, maybe she was doing a much better job of cleaning than usual, but she figured it wouldn't hurt to butter up her mom.

"Was that your friend Chelsea?" asked Mom.

Carlie gave the stove top one last swipe with the sponge. "Yeah."

"What did she want?"

Carlie wasn't sure how to put this and finally just spilled the beans about being invited for an overnight haircut-and-shopping trip to Portland. Then she held her breath, preparing herself for the worst.

"Maria told me that Mrs. Landers had mentioned something like that today. But do you really want to cut your hair, Carlotta?"

Carlie smiled hopefully. "I really do, Mom. I mean, it gets so hot, and then it gets tangled, and it takes so long to dry it. I would so love to have short hair."

Mom frowned as she ran her fingers through Carlie's long curls. "But I love your long hair, mija."

"I know."

"But my baby sister is probably right. You're growing up. I suppose you should be able to make some of your own decisions now."

"*Really?*" Carlie could hardly believe her ears. Was Mom agreeing to this?

Mom nodded. "If that's what you really want."

"*I do!*"

Mom sighed. "But let me take a picture of you before you get it cut."

Carlie laughed. "Oh, you already have lots of pictures, Mom."

"Still, I want one more."

So Carlie let her mom brush her hair and even tie a ribbon in it. Then they went outside and Carlie posed for her in her little garden, cooperating as Mom took several shots. Sure, it was silly, and Carlie would've been embarrassed if any of her friends had seen this, but it seemed a small price to pay to get her hair cut. She couldn't wait!

As soon as she got back in the house, she called Chelsea with the good news.

"That's great," said Chelsea. "And by the way, can you come over again tomorrow?"

"Sorry, but I just promised Mom that I'd stick around tomorrow."

"But I'll be so bored without you," complained Chelsea. "Can't you please come over? My mom said we could even pick you up."

"But I already told my mom I'd watch my brothers while she goes grocery shopping. And after she agreed to the haircut and trip to Portland, I can't really back out on her."

"How long can it take to get groceries?" asked Chelsea.

"With my mom it can take all morning."

"What about after that?" begged Chelsea.

"I already told my friends I'd hang with them here tomorrow afternoon."

"Oh…"

Now Carlie felt guilty. Maybe she should invite Chelsea to join them tomorrow. Still, she wasn't sure she was ready for that. And besides, she'd spent the past two days with Chelsea. "It's just one day," she told her. "And I can do something with you Thursday or Friday … and then we're going to Portland on Saturday and—"

"I know, but I just wanted you to come over tomorrow."

"But I can't."

"Is it because you don't like me?"

"Of course not," said Carlie. "We're friends, Chelsea."

"Just not as good of friends as those other girls?"

"No," insisted Carlie. "It's not like that. But I haven't spent any time with these guys lately … I think they're feeling snubbed."

"Yeah, well, I know just how they feel." And then Chelsea hung up on her. Just like that!

Carlie was stunned. What was she supposed to do? Should she call Chelsea back and apologize? But for what? Carlie hadn't done anything wrong. And yet she still felt guilty. She felt as if she owed Chelsea something. But why?

The next morning she still felt bad about Chelsea. She imagined her storming around in her spacious room, slamming doors and yelling at her poor mother — all because Carlie couldn't — or wouldn't — come over today. She actually picked up the phone, ready to call and apologize for hurting her feelings.

"Carlie!" yelled Miguel. "Pedro took my Batman car again, and he won't give it back to me!"

Carlie quickly realized she had no time to worry about Chelsea right now. And, she told herself as she extracted the coveted car from Pedro's chubby hands, if she wants to act like a spoiled brat, why should Carlie even care? She had her hands full with two other spoiled brats at the moment. Okay, maybe they weren't totally spoiled. But they sure knew how to act bratty sometimes. And this morning they were in top form.

She was so relieved when her mom came home.
"Thanks, mija," said Mom as she set the bags of groceries
on the counter. "You're free to go now."

"Thank you!" said Carlie. "And the boys should be
ready for a nap." And then she changed her grubby T-shirt
and ran over to the Rainbow Bus. It seemed like it had
been weeks since she'd been able to come here and hang
with her friends.

"This is so great!" she exclaimed as she entered the bus
and saw all three of her friends sitting at the little table.
"It's so good to be home again!"

They laughed and hugged her. "Welcome back," said
Morgan.

"We've missed you around here," said Emily. "The
club's just not the same with only three of us."

"Yeah," added Amy. "It's been too quiet."

"Well, I'm here now," said Carlie as she sank into the
plush-covered couch and sighed happily.

"By the way," said Amy. "I'm mad at you."

"Huh?" Carlie sat up and looked at Amy.

"Yeah, both my sisters told me that you brought your
new friend to the restaurant yesterday, and even introduced her to them, but then you didn't stick around long
enough for me to meet her too. Thanks a lot."

"Hey, it wasn't even two when we left. We would've
had to stay for more than an hour."

"You mean I'm not worth waiting for?" demanded Amy. Then she grinned. "Just kidding. An also told me that Chelsea lives at *Pacific Shores.*"

"Isn't that some fancy-dancy, ritzy neighborhood?" asked Morgan.

"It's pretty nice," admitted Carlie. Then she told them about the huge new house that overlooked the ocean and Chelsea's amazing bedroom and even the swimming pool.

"No way," said Amy. "She has a pool? A real in-ground pool?"

"Yep," said Carlie, leaning back into the couch again. "It even has this big fountain that flows right into it."

"No wonder you've been totally ignoring us," said Amy.

"I wasn't ignoring anyone," said Carlie. Then she told them about her little deals with Tia Maria.

Morgan laughed. "Well, I can't blame you for that. I would so hate it if my mom told me how to dress. And she actually has pretty good taste — for an old person anyway."

"Yeah, imagine how you'd feel if she wanted to dress you in ruffles and bows and lacy, pink foo-foo," said Carlie. "In middle school too!"

Morgan laughed. "That's pretty bad."

"But cutting your hair?" questioned Emily. "It's so pretty, Carlie. You really want to cut it?"

Carlie grabbed a handful of long curls and nodded eagerly. "Oh, yeah! I cannot wait to be rid of this. I'd whack it off right now if I could."

"Okay," said Morgan. "Since we're all here for the first time this week, I suggest we make this an official meeting."

"Official, huh?" teased Amy.

"You know what I mean." Morgan gave her a warning look. "We already told Carlie that we've discussed the possibility of having new members in our club."

"Yes," said Amy. "And we all agree it's a good idea."

"But we need to have a limit," said Emily. "This bus isn't exactly huge."

"That's right," agreed Morgan. "We think six girls would be plenty."

"And that's only because we probably wouldn't all be here at the same time that much anyway," said Emily.

"I suggested *eight* girls," said Amy. "That way we could each invite one."

"And we said we'd think about that idea," added Morgan. "The bigger question is how do we decide who can or cannot join?"

"Yes," said Emily. "It's not like we want to exclude anyone."

Morgan held up her hand with the rainbow bracelet. "After all, our motto is to love our neighbors as we love ourselves ... so we need to have open hearts."

"Still, we can't just let everyone in," said Emily.

"For starters they have to be girls and our age," said Morgan.

"Our same grade," Amy corrected her. "I mean, since Morgan is thirteen and I'm still eleven — but we're all going into seventh grade."

"And we talked about allowing only girls who live here in the trailer court," said Morgan.

"But then we realized there aren't any more," said Emily.

"Also," said Morgan, "we understand that you seem to be making friends with this Chelsea girl and she doesn't live here."

"Plus, limiting it to Harbor View does sound exclusive," said Amy.

Emily laughed. "Yes, this trailer court is *so exclusive!*"

"You know what I mean," said Amy.

"So anyway," concluded Morgan. "That's about as far as we've gotten. Do you think we should put it to a vote now that we're all here?"

"I move that we vote," said Amy.

"I guess I should be taking notes," said Emily as she reached for the notebook. "What exactly are we voting on anyway?"

"First of all, we'll vote whether or not we'll invite new members to join," said Morgan. "Then we'll vote as to how many more we think we can have."

So they voted and it was unanimous to expand their numbers by inviting others. The next vote — to limit it to only two more members — was passed three to one.

"It's just for the time being," Morgan assured Amy, the one opposing vote. "We can always decide to have more members later."

"Okay," agreed Amy. "It's not like girls are pounding down our doors to join up."

Morgan laughed. "I'm sure some girls would think our club was pretty corny."

"Too bad for them," said Emily as she closed the notebook. "They just don't know what they're missing."

"Speaking of that," said Morgan. "Should this be kind of a secret club?"

"What does that mean?" asked Carlie. "Because I already told Chelsea a little about it."

"Meaning that we don't talk about it," said Morgan, "you know, once school starts. We don't want to set ourselves up for trouble."

"Let's vote," said Amy.

"First let me explain my thoughts," said Morgan. "Like I said, it's not as if we want to exclude anyone. But the thing is if girls find out and are interested … well, how do we tell them they can't join?"

"Especially if we already have a full bus," said Emily.

"So I'm thinking we need to keep it quiet."

"Let's vote," said Amy again. And when they voted it was unanimous.

"But it's okay that I already told Chelsea?" asked Carlie.

"Yeah. And you can invite her to come visit," said Morgan.

"We want to meet her," said Emily.

So Carlie agreed to invite her. But she had to admit, if only to herself, it was a relief having a day off from Chelsea today. Sure, Chelsea was fun, but she could be difficult too. And even though the other girls seemed eager to meet her, Carlie wasn't so sure she was eager to have Chelsea meet them just yet. For now she was enjoying just hanging with her old friends.

chapter seven

That evening, Carlie started feeling guilty about Chelsea again. Maybe she should've called her and apologized earlier today. She looked at her club bracelet and realized she hadn't been exactly loving to Chelsea — not in the way that Carlie would want to be loved or treated. But, in all fairness, neither had Chelsea.

Carlie was heading for the phone when it rang, and — to her surprise — there was Chelsea on the other end. Carlie was about to invite Chelsea to come over and meet her friends, but she didn't get the chance.

"Hey, I'm sorry I hung up on you yesterday," said Chelsea quickly. "I know that was pretty childish on my part, but I just felt really left out."

"I'm sorry too, but I wanted to —"

"Anyway, before you brush me off again, I'm calling to invite you and your friends over to my house tomorrow. We'll just hang out and get to know each other. My mom will send out for pizza or something, and we can hang out by the pool and watch movies and whatever."

"That sounds great," said Carlie. "And I don't even have to babysit or anything tomorrow."

"And my mom can pick you guys up too," suggested Chelsea. "I mean, if you don't have a way to get over here. I'm thinking around eleven or so. Does that sound okay?"

Carlie considered the idea of Mrs. Landers and Chelsea driving their pretty Mercedes convertible into Harbor View Mobile-Home Court. And then she considered what their reaction might be to seeing where Carlie and her friends lived. Not that Carlie was ashamed of the trailer court — especially after they'd all worked so hard to fix it up — but it was so hugely different from what the Landers were used to. "How about if I see whether or not my friends can come first," she told Chelsea. "Then I'll call you back."

"Cool!"

So Carlie called the other three girls. All of them sounded very eager to meet Chelsea, and Amy couldn't wait to see her house.

"I can ask my grandma to take us over there," offered Morgan. "Since I know it's too far to walk."

"That'd be great," said Carlie with relief. At least this would postpone having Chelsea and her mom coming over here just yet. Even if it was shallow on her part, she just wasn't ready for that. So she called Chelsea and told her the good news.

"I'll see ya tomorrow then," said Carlie.

"Can't wait to meet your friends," said Chelsea.

Carlie felt more than a little nervous as Morgan's grandma drove them across town the next morning. She felt like crossing her fingers in the hopes that everything would go okay today.

"My aunt can give us a ride home," Carlie told Morgan's grandma as they got out of the car. "It'll be a tight squeeze, but we're not that big. I think we can all fit."

Carlie started to go into the house through the garage, but before she reached the side door, she heard Chelsea calling.

"Hey, you can use the front door," said Chelsea as she waved to the girls in the driveway. "Come on over here and enter the house like civilized folks."

Carlie laughed nervously as she walked over to Chelsea. Then trying to be polite, she started to introduce her friends.

"I already know who's who," interrupted Chelsea. She pointed to Morgan first. "You're Morgan, and I already met your mom down on the waterfront." Then she pointed at Amy. "You're Amy, and I met both your sisters at your family's restaurant." Finally she nodded to Emily. "And that means you're Emily."

"And you didn't meet any of my family?" teased Emily.

"Nope. Not yet anyway." Chelsea studied the four girls then smiled. "Well, come on in to my humble abode."

Carlie noticed Emily rolling her eyes, and Amy actually snickered.

"Thanks for inviting us over," said Morgan as they went inside. "This is a beautiful house, Chelsea."

"It's okay, I guess," said Chelsea in a tone that sounded like a cross between snobby and bored. "Our other house was lots nicer."

"Are you going to introduce me to your friends?" asked Mrs. Landers as she came down the stairs wearing a pale pink jogging suit. Carlie could tell Chelsea's mom was studying the girls carefully. And Carlie suspected by the slightly raised brows that she was surprised. But she just smiled politely as Chelsea did some quick introductions.

"So have you decided, Chelsea? Pizza or sub sandwiches or what for lunch?"

"Pizza?" asked Chelsea as she glanced at the others, and they nodded their approval.

"Good," said Mrs. Landers. "One-ish okay?"

"Sounds great," said Carlie.

"You girls have fun. I've got to run some errands. I'll call in the pizza while I'm out. And Maria is here if you need anything before I get back."

"Does she mean your aunt?" whispered Emily.

Carlie nodded, watching as Mrs. Landers whooshed away.

"Is Maria the maid?" asked Amy.

"Yes," said Chelsea.

"Not exactly," Carlie corrected her.

"Yes, she is," insisted Chelsea.

"Sure, she's been coming every day the past couple of weeks, but that's only to help them get settled and unpacked," explained Carlie. "After that, she'll come *once a week* to clean."

"Meaning that she's our maid," said Chelsea.

"She's your weekly cleaning lady," said Carlie.

Then Chelsea laughed. "See, you can tell we're old friends because we're already fighting half the time." The other girls laughed too. But Carlie didn't think it was all that funny.

"Your house is absolutely gorgeous," said Amy after Chelsea completed the full tour.

"That pool looks really nice too," said Emily. The five of them were standing around on the tiled deck now. Everyone seemed unsure of what to say or do next as they gazed out over the turquoise blue pool.

"There's a Jacuzzi too," said Chelsea, pointing to a smaller round pool off in the corner. "We'll use that more in the winter time. And my dad is going to put a pool table and some funky old video-game machines in the basement," she continued. "After it gets finished up down there."

"Cool!" said Amy with enthusiasm. Carlie could tell that Amy was really impressed by all this. But then who wouldn't be?

"Want to get on our suits and take a dip in the pool?" asked Chelsea.

"Sounds good to me," said Morgan, and the others agreed.

"Your bedroom is totally awesome," said Amy as the girls changed into their suits. "I would so love to live in a house like this."

"It's okay," said Chelsea.

"But your other room was lots nicer?" teased Carlie as she tugged on her swimsuit. She was getting tired of Chelsea's superior attitude.

"No." Chelsea firmly shook her head. "It wasn't nicer."

"Oh." Carlie felt dumb now.

"But I would've gladly stayed in my old room if we hadn't had to move here. I would've lived in the garage if that could've kept us from moving."

"So it was really hard on you?" asked Emily.

"Yeah," said Chelsea sadly. "We'd lived in Minneapolis my whole life, and I had to leave all my friends — even my very best friend — all back there."

"I kinda know how you feel," said Emily. "I moved here in June. Just before school ended. If I hadn't met Morgan and Carlie and Amy ... well, I'm sure I'd be really bummed by now."

"It must be so convenient having all your friends right there in your own neighborhood," said Chelsea as she adjusted a tie on her bathing suit bottom. "You just step out your door and there are your friends."

"Have you gotten to know any kids in your neighborhood yet?" asked Morgan. She already had on her swimsuit and was wrapping a brightly colored beach towel around her like a skirt.

Chelsea sighed. "No. Carlie's the only friend I've made."

"So far," said Amy with a bright smile. "But I think I can promise that we're all willing to be your friends too, Chelsea."

Carlie studied Amy for a long moment. As usual, Amy was wearing her cute little brightly colored two-piece. And, Carlie noticed, it wasn't so different from the one that Chelsea was tying around her own neck right now. Almost like these two girls could have something in common. Plus it was obvious that Amy was totally impressed by Chelsea's home and room and everything.

What if Amy was trying to take over here? What if she wanted to replace Carlie with herself in this pretty little picture? And even if she did want to do something like that, why should Carlie really care? But, to her surprise, Carlie thought maybe she did care.

She had to admit that she'd enjoyed having someone like Chelsea and her mother taking an interest in her. And she was actually looking forward to their trip to Portland this weekend. What if Chelsea suddenly decided she'd rather get haircuts with Amy? And what if she wanted to take Amy back-to-school shopping instead of Carlie? That would not be good!

chapter eight

As the girls hung together — swimming and splashing and joking and playing — Carlie worked hard to maintain her position as Chelsea's friend. Was she her *best* friend? Who could tell? But she went out of her way to say nice things to and about Chelsea. Still, the harder she tried, the less Chelsea seemed to notice her at all.

In fact, it seemed that most of Chelsea's attention was focused on Morgan just now. And Carlie almost got the feeling that Chelsea was testing her out.

"What's your dad do?" she asked Morgan as they were lounging around on the deck, drying in the sun.

"I don't know," said Morgan.

Chelsea looked shocked. "You don't know?"

All the girls got quiet now, as if they were holding their breaths so they could listen to her answer. As far as Carlie knew, Morgan had never mentioned her dad to any of them before. Of course, none of them had ever asked either.

"My parents split up when I was really little," said Morgan. "All I know is that my father was from New York and he was really into his music — more than he was into being a husband or a daddy."

"So you never see him?"

"Nope." Morgan rolled over onto her stomach, propping her chin in her hands. Carlie could tell that this was making her uncomfortable. But what was Chelsea's point?

"Was he black?" asked Chelsea. "Or African American? I mean, your skin doesn't seem as dark as your mom's, and I was —"

"Can you guys believe it's only *eleven days* until school starts?" said Carlie suddenly, making a feeble but desperate attempt to change the subject.

"I can't wait!" said Amy with real enthusiasm.

Carlie groaned. "That's right, Amy *loves* school! Can you believe it, Chelsea?"

"No way!" Chelsea turned her attention to Amy now. "Only geeks love school."

"She's not a geek," said Morgan in a flat voice.

"No, she's just a brainiac," teased Emily. "Ask her a math question and you'll see how fast she can answer it."

"I've heard that Asian kids are supposed to be really good in math," said Chelsea.

Amy seemed to bristle at this comment, but then she just smiled. "Well, your dad's a banker, Chelsea, I'd suppose you'd be good at math too."

Chelsea laughed. "Hardly."

"Well, if you ever need tutoring, you'll have to give me a call," offered Amy.

"Yeah, right." Now Chelsea reached over and flipped one of Morgan's braids. "How do you take care of these anyway?"

"Huh?" Morgan studied her for a moment.

"You know, how do you wash your hair and stuff?"

Morgan kind of laughed, but it didn't look like she thought it was funny. "Probably the same way you do, Chelsea, you know, with *shampoo and water.*"

"Hey, did I tell you guys I'm getting my hair cut?" asked Carlie, although she knew for a fact she had already told them.

"Yeah," said Emily quickly. "But you didn't say *how* you're getting it cut. What are you going to do anyway?"

"I'm not really sure," said Carlie. "I was thinking I should ask Morgan, since she's our local design and fashion expert."

Morgan brightened as she sat up and studied the shape of Carlie's face. "Well, you have kind of a heart-shaped face," she said as she pushed Carlie's wet hair back. "So maybe you shouldn't get it cut too short."

"Why not?" asked Chelsea quickly. "I think she'd look good with it short. And I'm going to get mine cut short. You know we're going to get our hair cut together."

"I know," said Morgan, not even looking at Chelsea. "But I think you'd look better with it coming just below your chin, Carlie. Maybe layered a little around your face to bring out your eyes."

Carlie nodded as she considered this. "But how am I going to remember how to explain that to the haircutter person?"

"We'll find a picture," said Morgan, "in a magazine."

"So how do you know so much about hair?" Chelsea asked Morgan with a creased brow, like she didn't really think Morgan knew what she was talking about.

Morgan just shrugged. "I pay attention to fashion. That's all."

"Well, so do I," said Chelsea. "And I think short hair would look totally cool on Carlie."

And suddenly the two of them started arguing about Carlie's hair. Carlie glanced nervously over at Emily and Amy, hoping they might help to end this craziness, but they looked just as surprised as she felt.

"Anyone want to run down to the beach?" asked Carlie, suddenly standing. "There's a trail nearby. I'll bet I can beat all of you guys down to the water!"

"I'll bet you can't," said Morgan, leaping to her feet.

Not waiting for anyone else to join, Carlie took off and Morgan was right on her heels. Carlie knew that she and Morgan were the fastest runners of the group and, as expected, they made it to the beach far ahead of the others, tying as they reached the surf.

"They're not even running," said Carlie as she looked back at the beach behind them.

"Wimps," said Morgan as she bent over to catch her breath.

"Hey, Morgan," said Carlie between breaths, "I'm sorry Chelsea is being so —"

"It's okay," said Morgan quickly. "No biggie."

"The first thing she told me about herself was that she has no impulse control. That means she just says whatever pops into her head without thinking whether or not it will hurt someone."

"I know," said Morgan. "Really, it's no big deal. Just chill, Carlie."

"Okay …"

Then Morgan waded out through the breaking waves until it got deep and she started to swim. Carlie followed her lead, watching as the other three girls slowly made their way over to the edge of the water. Soon all five of them were swimming and splashing in the waves, and Carlie told herself that whatever had happened back at Chelsea's house wasn't a big deal. Carlie had probably just made too much of it. She should take Morgan's advice and just chill.

Two pizzas had already arrived by the time the girls got back. Fortunately, Maria had put them in the oven to stay warm. The girls all jumped into the pool to rinse off the salt water and then sat around the deck munching on pizza and drinking soda. The dip in the ocean seemed to have cooled everyone off. And Carlie decided that her worries about Chelsea were probably silly. Even so, she was relieved when it was 4:30 and time to go home.

The girls all thanked Chelsea and her mother for everything, and Morgan invited Chelsea to come spend the day with them sometime.

"You can see our clubhouse and our beach," she said with a smile.

"How about tomorrow?" asked Chelsea.

Morgan looked slightly surprised. "It works for me," she said, glancing at the others.

"I'll be around until three," said Amy. She frowned. "Then I have to go work at the restaurant. Friday is one of its busy nights."

"I'm always around," said Emily.

"I'll be free," said Carlie. "Unless I have to babysit. But Mom hasn't mentioned it."

"So tomorrow then?" said Chelsea.

"Come in the morning," said Amy eagerly. "So I'll have more time to spend with you before I have to leave."

"How about ten-ish?" asked Chelsea.

"Sounds great," said Morgan with a bright smile.

As they rode home, Carlie wondered if Morgan was as happy as she acted about tomorrow's plans. But Carlie wouldn't question her. She sensed that she'd already offended Morgan by being too concerned about Chelsea's behavior today. Besides, Morgan was a strong person. She could speak up if she needed to. Even so, Carlie felt guilty as she went into her house. It seemed that her connection to Chelsea could go either way. Why did it have to get so complicated?

"Friend trouble?" asked Tia Maria as Carlie walked through the kitchen.

"What?" asked Mom with a concerned frown.

"Our Carlie is such a popular girl," said her aunt with a wink. "I think some of her friends are fighting over her now."

"Not really," said Carlie, wondering where her aunt was getting her information or, rather, misinformation.

"Just be good to your friends," said Mom, "and they will be good to you."

Carlie nodded, telling herself that her mom didn't understand either. If only it was that simple. "I'm going to dump my stuff in my room," she said, eager to escape their weird comments.

"Rinse the chlorine out of your swimsuit before you hang it to dry," warned Mom.

Carlie was barely in her room when she heard the phone ringing.

"It's Chelsea Landers," said Mom, handing her the cordless phone. "Keep it short. Your dad is supposed to call soon."

"Hi, Chelsea," said Carlie without much enthusiasm.

"I'm sorry," began Chelsea. "I made a complete mess of things today, didn't I?"

"Oh, I don't know …"

"Yes, *you do too know*. And I totally did. I stuck my foot in my mouth again. I offended Morgan. And I probably offended you too. I'm such a social freak sometimes."

Suddenly Carlie felt sorry for Chelsea. "No, you're not. It's just that you don't know my friends very well … and then you sometimes talk without thinking."

"I know. I know. It's that old no-impulse-control thing. I'm such a loser, Carlie. I'll probably totally bomb at school. Oh, help me, please. *Please!*"

"Look, I'm not supposed to be on the phone too long. My dad's going to call and —"

"You don't have call waiting?"

"No." Carlie took in a quick breath. Did Chelsea think everyone was made of money? "But listen, Chelsea, just try to chill, okay? When you come here tomorrow, don't try so hard with my friends. And don't turn everything into a stupid fight, okay?"

"Okay."

"And just be yourself, Chelsea. I mean, you're a cool girl and I do like you. But you can come on kinda strong sometimes. Just try to relax and it'll probably go okay."

"Okay."

"Now I gotta go."

"Thanks, Carlie. You're my best friend."

"What about Audrey?"

"Well, she *used* to be my best friend. But, as you know, that's all over with. Now you're my best friend. Is that okay with you?"

"Sure," said Carlie. She wanted to reassure Chelsea that she was her best friend too, but somehow she couldn't bring herself to say those words just yet. "See ya tomorrow, okay?"

"Okay. And I promise to behave better."

Carlie laughed. "Well, don't be too good. That'd be boring, not to mention weird."

She hung up the phone and went outside to water her garden. It was weird thinking that Chelsea considered her to be her best friend now, especially after they'd known each other only a few days. Still, Carlie had been wanting a best friend for months.

Carlie had already accepted that Morgan and Emily were best friends. Not that they ever said it. But it seemed like they shared something that Carlie was totally missing. Maybe it was because they were both Christians and went to the same church. And while Carlie considered herself a good Catholic, she still felt maybe she was different than them — like maybe she didn't really get it.

She bent down to pull out a few small weeds that had sneaked into her petunias. Maybe that was why she got paired off with Amy most of the time. Because in some ways it seemed like Amy didn't get it either. And while Amy was nice enough, not to mention super smart, she sometimes got on Carlie's nerves with all her "Little Miss Perfect" kind of talk. Besides that, Amy just didn't seem to get Carlie most of the time. Or maybe Carlie just didn't get Amy.

Even so, Carlie wasn't totally convinced that Chelsea would make a *better* best friend than Amy. In fact, Chelsea kind of scared Carlie sometimes. *Still,* she told herself, *maybe any best friend was better than none.* Especially when you were about to start seventh grade in a town where you only knew a few kids anyway. Maybe Carlie couldn't afford to be too picky when it came to best friends.

chapter nine

Carlie tried not to wig out over the idea of Chelsea and her mom coming to the trailer court this morning. She tried not to imagine their shocked faces when they drove up to her house, so totally different from what they were used to. Still it was all she could think about. *Okay, don't blow this all out of proportion,* she told herself as she went outside. *Just chill.*

She went out to her garden to distract herself by watering her flowers and picking off dried up blooms. Usually her garden cheered her up, but today she could only see it through the Landers' eyes. It was so small and frumpy compared to their big landscaped yard. And the little fountain she and her dad had worked hard to make suddenly looked so ordinary as she remembered the Landers' luxurious swimming pool and the massive fountain that flowed into it.

"Carlotta?" called her mom from the backdoor. "Your friends are here."

Carlie turned off the hose and hurried back into the house. It looked so weird to see both Chelsea and Mrs. Landers standing in the center of her living room. Chelsea's mom looked totally out of place in her sleek white pantsuit, but Carlie's mom just smiled at her as if all this was perfectly normal. Carlie desperately hoped that Pedro wouldn't suddenly dash around the corner with jam-smeared hands to wipe on those perfectly white pants.

"I was just telling your mother about our plans for the trip to Portland," said Mrs. Landers. She handed Carlie's mom a piece of notepaper. "Here are the phone numbers and whatnot, in case you should need to reach us."

"Thank you," said Carlie's mom. "It's so nice of you to invite Carlotta to go with you this weekend."

Mrs. Landers smiled at Carlie. "So your name is really *Carlotta?*"

Carlie sighed. "Only Mom calls me that."

"But it is your name, mija," her mother reminded her.

"Yeah, yeah." Carlie turned to Chelsea now. "Want to see my garden?"

"You have a garden?" asked Chelsea.

Carlie nodded as she tugged Chelsea through the kitchen and toward the backdoor. "Yeah, it's out here."

"Bye, girls," called Mrs. Landers. "Call me when you want to be picked up, Chelsea."

"I will."

"Have fun!"

"This is it," said Carlie once she and Chelsea were outside. She gave her friend a quick tour, telling her the names of the flowers and showing her the fountain and the planter boxes she'd helped Dad make.

"It's pretty small back here," said Chelsea.

Carlie nodded. "Yeah, I guess so."

"But it's pretty," said Chelsea.

"Really?" Carlie felt hopeful. "You really think so?"

"Yeah. I'm impressed you know how to do this. We have landscapers that come and take care of all this stuff for us."

"I know ... " Carlie held her chin up now. "I want to be a landscape designer some day. I'll have my own business."

Chelsea looked surprised. "You'd want to go and work in people's yards when you're a grown-up?"

"I'd have people working for me," she said quickly. "Not that I wouldn't do the dirty work too. I don't mind getting my hands dirty."

Chelsea laughed. "You're a funny girl, Carlie."

"Yeah, whatever ... "

"Hey, where's this cool clubhouse you and your friends keep talking about? Do I get to see it or not?"

"Of course," said Carlie as she opened the little gate from her garden. "It's down this way and—"

"Hey," called Amy, waving from across the street. "I thought that must've been Chelsea's car leaving just now. You guys heading over to the Rainbow Bus?"

"Rainbow Bus?" echoed Chelsea. "That sounds like a kiddies show on public TV. Is Barney there? Or maybe the Teletubbies?"

Amy laughed. "No, we're a little more sophisticated than that."

Carlie didn't say anything as they walked down the path toward the beach. Mostly she wished that they'd never invited Chelsea to come here. She saw Morgan and Emily up ahead, waiting for them where the trail forked off to the bus.

"Hey, you guys," said Morgan as they joined them. "Before we take Chelsea to the clubhouse, we need to make sure she understands some things. Okay?"

"Like what?" asked Chelsea with a suspicious look.

"Well, we need to know we can trust you," said Morgan.

"Why?"

"Because we don't want everyone finding out about our clubhouse, particularly where it's located. It's kind of a secret."

"And we had a little trouble with some boys earlier this summer," said Emily. "We wouldn't want any of them to know about this place."

"Well, Derrick Smith is in juvenile detention anyway," said Amy. "I don't think we need to worry about—"

"I don't even know anyone in town besides you guys," Chelsea pointed out. "Who am I going to tell?"

"That's right," said Amy quickly. "Lighten up, Morgan."

"We just need to be careful," said Morgan.

"That's right," agreed Emily.

"And we need to know we can trust Chelsea."

"So what do you want me to do?" asked Chelsea. "You want me to sign my name in blood? Or swear on a Bible? Or what?"

Morgan laughed. "We just want your word. Just promise that you'll respect our secret and you can see the clubhouse."

Chelsea held up her hand like she was taking an oath. "I promise I won't tell anyone."

"Good." Morgan nodded. "That works."

"Right this way," said Emily. The five girls all turned onto the path that led to the bus.

"Whoa," said Chelsea when she saw the bus. "It does sort of look like a rainbow."

"Yep," said Morgan as she unlocked the door. "It's our own little rainbow."

"Wait until you see the inside," said Emily, stepping aside so that Chelsea could go in behind Morgan.

"Morgan's our designer," said Carlie as she followed Chelsea in. She hoped that Chelsea wouldn't say anything mean. You could never tell with this girl.

"This is pretty cool," said Chelsea as she looked around the bus. "Kind of retro, huh?"

"Yeah," said Morgan. "It went with the whole style of the bus."

Chelsea sat down on the plush-covered couch. "I like it."

Carlie let out a small sigh of relief as she sat down beside her. Then Morgan turned on the old record player and put an old Beatles album on. Amy plugged in the string of fruit lights to give the place a festive feel. And Emily opened the little fridge. "We have juice or soda," she said. "Want anything, Chelsea?"

"And lunch will be catered today," said Morgan.

"Really?" Carlie looked curiously at Morgan. She hadn't heard anything about this.

Morgan grinned. "Grandma offered."

Carlie realized that her three friends had all gone out of their way to make this visit with Chelsea special. And it made her feel warm inside.

They talked and played music and before long it was noon. Morgan and Emily ran back to Morgan's house to get their "catered" lunch.

"This is really a cool place to hang with your friends," said Chelsea as she checked things out more closely.

"We like it," said Amy as she began to set plates and napkins on the small table, getting it ready for lunch.

"You could have good parties here," said Chelsea.

"Parties?" asked Carlie.

"You know, boy-girl parties."

Amy giggled. "Well, we haven't made an official rule about it yet, but I have a strong suspicion there will be no boys allowed."

"No boys?" Chelsea looked surprised. "*Not ever?*"

"It's a girls-only club," said Carlie. "We like it like that."

Chelsea laughed. "Well, you might not always think that way."

"Here's lunch," said Morgan as she and Emily came back in with a bag and cardboard box. Soon it was neatly arranged on the table, and after Morgan said a blessing, they began to eat.

"So is this a *Christian* club?" asked Chelsea as she reached for a handful of potato chips.

Carlie glanced at Morgan, wondering how she would answer this.

"Some of us are Christians," said Morgan. "But it's not a requirement."

"Are you a Christian, Amy?" asked Chelsea. "I mean, I thought oriental people were Buddhists or something like that."

"My parents used to practice Buddhism," said Amy in a slightly defensive tone. "But I think they gave it up when they moved to America. My sister An is a Christian though."

"She is?" said Morgan with interest.

Amy nodded. "Yes. My parents aren't too happy about it."

"Oh."

"How about you, Carlie?" asked Chelsea. "Are you a Christian?"

Carlie considered this. "Well, I … yeah … I guess."

"But like I said," Morgan jumped in. "You don't have to be a Christian to belong in this club. But you do have to agree to certain things." Then she held up her rainbow bracelet. "Rainbows rule."

The other girls held up theirs too, echoing her.

"So what's the deal with those bracelets?" asked Chelsea. "What do the letters mean?"

"Carlie didn't tell you?" asked Amy.

"No way," said Carlie. "Morgan said it was a secret, remember?"

"I don't remember her saying that," said Amy.

"Well, she did," said Emily. "I suppose you've told someone by now."

"No, I haven't," said Amy.

"It's kind of our code," said Morgan. "If you become a member, we'll tell you what it means."

"Meaning I could become a member?" asked Chelsea.

"Sure," said Amy. "We've already been discussing it."

Chelsea frowned now. "But I might not want to … "

"No one's going to force you," said Carlie. Feeling irritated, she got up and went over to the record player, carefully flipping the record over and placing the needle on the edge. Then she sat down in the driver's seat and just looked out the window, out toward where the ocean was, although it was hidden by the tall beach grass that grew in the dunes. She listened as the girls continued talking. And it seemed that Chelsea was trying to be a little nicer. Maybe she realized that Carlie was getting fed up with her little jabs and barbs.

"So what are we going to do now?" asked Chelsea after they cleaned up the lunch things.

"We could go to the beach," suggested Morgan. "That morning fog has finally burned off."

"Yeah, we could catch some sun," said Emily. "My tan's starting to fade."

Chelsea laughed. "And in this club, a girl needs a good tan to fit in."

"That's not true," snapped Carlie, instantly sorry that she did.

"Don't be so touchy," said Chelsea. "I'm just kidding."

"Let's get our suits," suggested Morgan as she headed for the door. "We might want to take a swim."

"I didn't bring mine," said Chelsea.

"I have an extra one," said Carlie reluctantly.

"I'll bet it's not a bikini," teased Chelsea.

"That's right," said Carlie. "My mom would kill me if I wore a bikini."

"I could loan you a bathing suit," offered Amy.

Chelsea laughed. "Yeah, but it would be a teeny-weeny bikini, and I'm not sure that I'm ready to show that much skin."

Carlie had stayed up late last night, carefully cleaning her room, just in case Chelsea needed to see it. But as they walked into her house, she realized that it made no difference. Chelsea would probably still find lots to make fun of in there. Carlie braced herself as she held the door open for Chelsea.

"Everything is so small here," said Chelsea, looking around the tiny, crowded space. "It's like a midget house."

"Except that we're not midgets," said Carlie as she pulled out her two swimsuits. "Take your pick."

Naturally, Chelsea picked Carlie's favorite, the bright orange tankini. "It's not exactly my style," said Chelsea. "But I guess it'll have to do."

Carlie took the other suit and began tugging it on. It had navy and white stripes and was getting a little small. She'd had it since fifth grade and hoped she wouldn't split a seam in it today. Just to be safe she pulled a pair of nylon shorts on over it.

"Being modest, are we?" teased Chelsea.

"No," admitted Carlie. "But this suit is getting a little tight."

Chelsea nodded. "You really should get a two-piece, Carlie. You would look totally awesome in one."

Carlie smiled. "Yeah, but I'd be toast if Mom saw me."

Chelsea rolled her eyes. "Your mom is so old-fashioned."

"Tell me about it."

Carlie grabbed a couple of towels. Not the big, fluffy, pool towels like they used at Chelsea's house, but at least she picked out ones that weren't too faded or frayed.

The girls met at the clubhouse and then walked down to the beach, laughing and joking as they went. It actually seemed like everyone was accepting Chelsea — and like Chelsea was trying to fit in. And yet, Carlie still felt a strained awkwardness. Or maybe she was just being too sensitive. But she felt responsible for Chelsea. Like if Chelsea said or did something to offend one of her friends, it would be Carlie's fault.

They went to their favorite part of the beach, where it was slightly sheltered in case the wind picked up. They began to arrange their towels and blankets, making themselves comfortable.

"I wish I brought my iPod," said Chelsea. "Then we could have some music."

"You have an iPod?" said Amy.

"Yeah. And it's loaded with tunes."

"You are so lucky."

"I'm curious, Chelsea," said Morgan as she rolled a sweatshirt up like a pillow and placed it beneath her head. "You asked about this being a Christian club ... does that mean you're a Christian?"

"Not hardly," said Chelsea.

"Then why did you ask?"

"Because you girls seem kind of like that."

"Kind of like that?" Morgan turned her head and peered at Chelsea from beneath her oversized sunglasses. "What does that mean?"

"Oh, you know … goody-goody … nicey-nice."

"Oh … "

"Well, I'm a Christian," said Emily. "And I'm not exactly goody-goody." She laughed. "Of course, I haven't been a Christian for very long. I've still got a lot to learn, huh, Morgan?"

Morgan sat up and shrugged. "I don't know … I think you're doing just fine, Emily."

"So you're the strong Christian in the group?" said Chelsea. "I knew it."

"Strong Christian?" echoed Morgan. "You mean like I probably pump iron while I read the Bible?"

Everyone but Chelsea laughed.

"No, I mean the kind of Christian who looks down on everyone who's *not* saved like her."

"Morgan doesn't do that!" Emily sat up on her knees and planted her hands on her hips.

"That's right," said Carlie. "Not at all."

"I think she does." Chelsea sat up now. "I think she looks down on me."

"Where do you get that nonsense?" demanded Emily. "Morgan isn't like that at all. Not with anyone!"

"Hey," said Morgan. "Calm down, you guys. If Chelsea really thinks those things, I'd like to hear why."

"Yeah, *why*?" said Emily, still visibly mad.

Chelsea shrugged. "I just get that feeling."

"*What* feeling?" Emily stared at Chelsea.

"You know, like she thinks she's so superior. It's just like the Christian girls at my other school. Audrey and I used to make fun of them all the time."

"You made fun of them?" asked Morgan. "Just because they were Christians?"

"Because they were freaks," said Chelsea. "They always talked about who was saved and who wasn't saved and how they were praying for everyone and everything — always acting like they were better than everyone else."

"But Morgan's not like that," said Carlie.

"She's not," admitted Amy. "I mean, she and I don't always agree on stuff, but Morgan has never put anyone down for not being a Christian."

Chelsea just shrugged again. "Well, maybe I'm wrong. You guys don't have to get all mad about it."

Morgan smiled at her. "I'm not mad, Chelsea. I was just curious. The thing is I really don't want to come across as that kind of person. I believe that Jesus was the most accepting and loving person to ever walk the planet. If anything, I want to be more like him."

"Well, the Christians at my other school were not accepting or loving," said Chelsea. "Not even close."

"Maybe it's because you teased them," said Emily.

Chelsea didn't say anything.

"I don't know about you guys," said Carlie. "But I am getting way too hot in the sun. I'm going in for a swim." Then she took off, marching toward the water. She knew the real reason she was getting hot was because of Chelsea. Why did that girl have to poke and prod and get everyone mad at her all the time? At this rate, she doubted that anyone would want to invite her to join the club. And maybe that was for the best.

"Hey, Carlie," called Chelsea, coming up from behind. "Did I do it again?"

"Huh?" Carlie just looked at her, trying to pretend like nothing was wrong.

"You know what I mean. I stuck my foot in my mouth with Morgan. And now you're mad at me? Right?"

Carlie shrugged. "I don't know ... "

"Well, if it makes you feel any better, I told Morgan I was sorry and she said it was no problem. She said she liked having conversations like that. She said it made her think about things."

Carlie nodded as she went beyond the next set of waves. "Well, good. I'm glad you guys don't hate each other."

"But you're still mad at me?"

Carlie turned and looked at Chelsea to see that her friend did look truly sorry. "No," said Carlie. "I'm not mad. But you're a funny girl, Chelsea Landers."

"Let's see who can swim the farthest," said Chelsea as she raced into the deeper water and then dove in and started to swim.

Carlie followed. And after she recovered from the jolt of cold on her sun-baked head, she told herself that she probably was overreacting to everything. Chelsea was just a normal girl who happened to like speaking her mind. Really, what was wrong with that?

To Carlie's relief, no decisions were made about whether or not Chelsea would be invited to join their club on Friday. In fact, other than the one time that morning, the subject hadn't even come up again. And it occurred to Carlie that Chelsea might not even be interested.

"You have everything you need, Carlotta?" Mom asked for like the umpteenth time that morning.

"Yes, Mom." Carlie rinsed her cereal bowl and placed it in the dishwasher. "I told you, I'm all packed and ready to go."

"And you'll call me if you need anything?"

"And you'd hop in the car and bring it to me?" teased Carlie.

"You know what I mean."

"I'll be fine, Mom," Carlie promised. "Don't worry."

"I am worried," said Mom. "I don't like the idea of you carrying all that money around in your purse while you girls are in the city."

"Like Dad suggested," Carlie reminded her, "I'll ask Mrs. Landers to hold on to some of it for me."

"Oh, yes." Mom nodded.

"They're here," said Carlie. She bent down and kissed Mom and then ran to get her bags. She wished that Mom would stay here in the kitchen with the boys, but as expected, she followed Carlie out to the driveway where Chelsea and her mom had just pulled up in the Mercedes.

Still wearing her frumpy pink robe and with Pedro now tugging on her sleeve, Mom stood on the edge of the driveway and waved as Carlie got into the backseat of the car. Carlie waved back, relieved that Mrs. Landers was already backing out.

"It must be a challenge having two small boys so close in age," said Mrs. Landers as she drove out onto the street.

"They can be a handful," admitted Carlie.

"I brought a bunch of new magazines," said Chelsea. "I thought we could get some ideas for things we want to shop for." She opened one magazine to a page with a Post-it note. "This is how I want my hair cut."

"That's cute," said Carlie.

"Why don't you get yours cut the same?" asked Chelsea.

"I have a magazine picture in here." Carlie opened her purse and pulled out the piece of paper and showed it to her. "Morgan found it for me. It's a little longer than the one you have though."

"But you'd look so cool with it cut like this," insisted Chelsea.

They went back and forth about it for a while, and finally Carlie said she'd think about it. "Let's look at clothes now," she suggested. "Show me the things that you think will look good on us."

So for the next couple of hours they studied the fashion magazines and listened to music from Chelsea's iPod. Carlie knew this was going to be a very good trip after all.

"Now don't let Chelsea influence you, Carlie," said Mrs. Landers as she took them into a very fancy hair salon. "You get your hair cut the way you want it."

"Thanks a lot, Mom," said Chelsea with a frown.

Carlie winked at Mrs. Landers. "Thanks!"

"I'm getting a manicure," she told them. "I'll be over there when you're done."

Carlie felt nervous as she got into the haircutting chair, but she forced a smile as Shari, the beautician, wrapped a purple cape around her shoulders.

Shari lifted Carlie's curls out of the cape. "Beautiful hair," she told her as she fingered the long, dark curls.

Carlie frowned.

"But you want it cut?"

"Yes." Carlie produced the slightly rumpled photo from the magazine.

Shari nodded. "Yes, this would look good on you."

"I'm just so tired of all this hair," Carlie told her. "It's everywhere and it gets in everything."

Shari laughed. "Do you mind if I measure it?"

"Measure it?"

"Yes. If we can take off ten inches, you could donate it to Locks of Love … if you wanted to."

"Locks of Love?"

"They make wigs for cancer patients who lose their hair from chemotherapy."

"Oh." Carlie nodded. "I hope there's enough."

As it turned out, there was enough. "Look," said Shari, holding up the long, curly ponytail. "You're going to make someone very happy with this."

"Good," said Carlie, but all she could do was stare at her reflection in the mirror. Her hair was sticking out like an overgrown bush. She was afraid she was going to cry. Maybe her mom was right!

"Don't worry," said Shari. "It's going to look great when I'm done."

"Do you mind if I close my eyes?"

Shari laughed. "Not at all."

So Carlie shut her eyes and waited while Shari snipped and snipped with her scissors. Finally, she told Carlie she was finished.

Carlie took in a deep breath before she opened her eyes, but when she did, she was relieved. It did look better. In fact, it looked great.

"That's perfect!" she told Shari. "Thank you so much!" She reached up and patted her hair. "And it feels so good.

So much lighter."

Shari gave her some tips for how to keep it looking good, then Mrs. Landers insisted on paying for both girls' haircuts.

"But I have my own money," said Carlie.

"I know," said Mrs. Landers. "But I'd like to do this for you."

Carlie thanked her, but she wished that she had paid for it herself.

"You'll have more money for clothes now," Chelsea told her as they got in the car.

"Your hair looks so cute," said Carlie. "It's perfect on you."

"I have to admit yours looks good too," said Chelsea. "But I think you'd look just as good if it was shorter."

The next stop was a large mall. First they got a quick lunch, then Mrs. Landers walked them around a bit until they all knew the basic layout of the shops and department stores. "I'm going to meet my friend Leslie at Starbucks for coffee," she told them. "Chelsea, you have your phone and I have mine. Check in with me in about an hour, okay?"

Then, just like that, Chelsea and Carlie were totally on their own. It made Carlie a little nervous at first, but at the same time it made her feel much older too. "Does your mom let you shop by yourself all the time?" she asked as they went into an American Eagle store.

"Only if I'm with a friend," said Chelsea. "Hey, look at this." She held up a pair of khaki pants. "These are so cool."

Soon they both had a pile of things to try on. And by the time they left the store, Carlie had spent nearly $100. "Wow," said Carlie. "I never spent that much money on clothes before." She didn't admit that it concerned her that she'd only purchased four items of clothing and three of them were just T-shirts.

"You're going to look so cool when school starts," said Chelsea as they walked to the next store.

"I'm going to have to get some more of my money from your mom," said Carlie.

"I told you to keep it with you," said Chelsea. "Money goes fast when you're at the mall."

"Well, my parents were worried … they thought I'd get mugged or something."

Chelsea laughed. "Yeah, right."

Carlie did run out of money at the third store. But Chelsea loaned her enough to get the jeans she wanted, and then they met up with her mom and Leslie at Starbucks.

"Can we leave our bags with you?" asked Chelsea.

"You girls look like you've got this shopping thing down," said Leslie.

"Chelsea is showing me how it works," Carlie admitted as Mrs. Landers gave her the rest of her money.

"Well, Chelsea was trained by the best," said Leslie, winking at Mrs. Landers.

"I hope I can keep up," said Carlie.

"Here," said Mrs. Landers to Chelsea. "I'll let you take my Nordstrom's card with you. Just in case you run out of cash."

"Thanks!"

They shopped and shopped, and Carlie was actually starting to get tired. Plus her eyes were burning and her ears were ringing. She wondered how Chelsea managed to keep going.

"We still need to look at shoes," said Chelsea. So Carlie trudged after her into a shoe store. After they tried on several pairs, Chelsea told Carlie which ones to get.

"You're sure?" asked Carlie, looking at the price.

"Yep. Those are totally cool."

So, knowing that she was using the last of her money, Carlie got the shoes. "That does it for me," she said as the saleswoman handed her the bag.

"What?" said Chelsea.

"I'm out of money," said Carlie. "So I'm done."

Chelsea frowned. "Well, I'm not."

Carlie held up all the bags. Some of them were cutting into her hands. "I'm tired."

"Let's drop them off with Mom. And then you can help me to finish up. I still need to find a jacket and some shoes and … "

Carlie let the rest of the list just float over her as they went back to Starbucks and dumped the rest of their bags on Mrs. Landers and Leslie.

"Aren't you girls ready to go yet?" she asked Chelsea.

"Just another hour, Mom," she pleaded.

"Then we're leaving," warned her mom.

"No problem."

Carlie followed Chelsea around, waiting as she tried on still more clothes and helping her carry packages.

"I'm out of money too," said Chelsea just as they stopped in front of an accessories shop.

"Then let's go," said Carlie, relieved that this shopping madness was coming to an end.

"But I need a necklace to go with that peach-colored top I just got."

"But you're out of money."

"I can look, can't I?"

"What's the point?" asked Carlie.

"I *need* a necklace."

"Well, you've still got your mom's Nordstrom's card. You could go there for a necklace."

"That's clear at the other end of the mall." Chelsea looked at her watch. "We don't have time."

"But you don't have money," Carlie reminded her as Chelsea stubbornly walked into the small shop.

Carlie rearranged the bags she was carrying for Chelsea so she could get through the tight aisles that were filled with racks and racks of earrings and pendants and bracelets. Why was Chelsea wasting time here anyway? Carlie took a deep breath, reassuring herself that soon it would be time to go, and this never-ending shopping excursion would come to an end. She glanced over at one of the many mirrors in this shop and was surprised to see a girl with cute dark hair that was cut in layers around her face. Then she realized it was her and almost laughed. Almost. Because she saw something else in the mirror just then. In that same instant, she saw Chelsea behind her, and she was swooping several necklaces right off the rack and into her opened Banana Republic bag. Just like that. Chelsea wasn't even looking at the things that tumbled into her bag — almost as if she didn't know it had happened. But Carlie knew that she did.

First Carlie started to turn around to tell her to put them back. But then Carlie got scared. What would happen if she was caught with Chelsea? Would she get in trouble too? Carlie glanced over to where the door was — just a few feet away from her. And then without even looking at Chelsea, she turned and walked out of the store.

Her heart was pounding hard as she went back out into the mall. She walked a few shops down, trying to distance herself from the shop — and Chelsea. She couldn't believe that she'd just seen what she felt certain she had seen. Why would Chelsea do that? Her parents were so rich, she could easily afford to buy half the things in that shop. Why would she take such a chance?

"Why did you run off?" asked Chelsea, coming up from behind Carlie.

"I saw what you did," said Carlie.

Chelsea laughed. "So?"

"You stole those necklaces, Chelsea."

"It's no biggie." She glanced over her shoulder now. "Come on, it's time to go."

"But it was wrong," said Carlie as they walked down the mall. Carlie's heart was still pounding hard. She felt guilty too. As if she were as much to blame as Chelsea. She also felt certain that they would both be arrested at any moment.

Somehow they made it to Starbucks without being stopped, but Carlie felt certain they wouldn't make it out of the mall. She knew that shops had security cameras — especially the stores where teenagers shopped. She'd seen it on TV.

"At last," said Mrs. Landers, standing. "Leslie took off already. I talked her into taking some of your bags with her. We can sort them all out when we get to her house." She glanced at Carlie now. "Are you feeling okay, Carlie? You don't look well."

"I wore her out," said Chelsea. "She's not used to this."

"Poor Carlie," said Mrs. Landers. "We should've warned you."

Yeah, thought Carlie, *they should've!*

They piled all the bags into the trunk of the car, but Chelsea kept the Banana Republic bag with her. Carlie wondered if she was finally feeling guilty for her stupidity. Maybe she was going to ask her mom if she could take it back.

"I got you something, Carlie," she said loudly enough for her mom to hear. "Let me try it on you." Then she pulled out a beaded necklace with pale blue beads. It was actually very pretty. "This will be perfect with that blue top you got at the Gap." Then she put it around Carlie's neck and fastened it. "Oh, it looks great with your haircut too."

Mrs. Landers turned around to see and then smiled. "Yes, it does look lovely on you, Carlie. Chelsea has such good taste."

Carlie didn't say anything. She was too angry!

chapter eleven

"Are you going to be mad forever?" asked Chelsea as the two girls sat and watched a movie in the family room at Leslie's house.

"Maybe," said Carlie.

"Like I already told you, I'm sorry," said Chelsea. "I made a mistake. Remember the no-impulse-control thing? I guess it just ran away with me this afternoon."

"You did it on purpose," said Carlie. "You knew exactly what you were doing."

"It doesn't matter," said Chelsea. "Like I told you, those shops have insurance for theft. We're the ones who pay for it too. All the things we bought today cover the cost of insurance. It's no big deal."

"It's stealing."

"Shhh … "

"I'm going to bed," said Carlie, standing.

"Well, I'm going to watch the rest of the movie."

So Carlie went upstairs and was just turning to go down the hallway when she heard Leslie and Mrs. Landers talking. They were sitting by the big window that over-looked the city lights. But they couldn't see her.

"The truth is I feel sorry for Carlie," said Mrs. Landers. "She and her other little friends live in this pathetic little trailer park on the bad side of town. Everyone there is so poor. And Chelsea told me they have this sad little club. I swear it's like an ethnic potluck. One girl is black, one is Chinese, and then there's our little Carlie." She laughed. "It's actually rather funny. I mean, to think of where we came from and the kinds of kids that Chelsea is used to being friends with."

"You sound like a snob," said Leslie.

"Oh, I don't mean to," said Mrs. Landers. "I really do like Carlie. And her aunt has been such a godsend, helping me to get settled into the house and all. But I expect that Chelsea will move on to some more appropriate friends, you know, once school starts ..."

"So she's just using Carlie?"

"Oh, Leslie, you make it sound so cheap and mean."

"Isn't it?"

"Carlie already has her friends. Like I said, she has the trailer-park kids. I'm sure she won't even feel bad when Chelsea moves on."

"But what if she does?"

"Well, I suppose we could work on Carlie. Help her to make more of herself. She's a pretty girl. And she seems smart enough. And she does have good manners."

Leslie laughed. "And perhaps you could groom her into something acceptable."

"You make me sound like a monster."

Carlie tiptoed down the hallway to the bedroom that Leslie had given her and Chelsea to share tonight. Blinking back tears, Carlie pulled on her pajamas and climbed into one of the twin beds. But it was a long time before she went to sleep.

"You're being awfully quiet, Carlie," said Mrs. Landers as the three of them drove home on Sunday. "Are you feeling okay?"

"I'm fine," said Carlie. "Just worn out, I guess."

"Yeah," said Chelsea. "Our little shopathon was too much for the poor girl."

Carlie rolled her eyes and leaned back into the seat. The sooner she got home, the happier she'd be. She decided to pretend to be sleeping as they drove. To her surprise, she actually fell asleep and had to be awakened in her own driveway.

"Wake up, sleepyhead," said Chelsea. "You're home."

Chelsea helped Carlie carry her packages up to the front porch. "Like I said, I'm sorry," she told her. "I hope you won't hate me forever."

"I don't hate you," said Carlie. She waved and called out thanks to Mrs. Landers.

"I'll call you," said Chelsea.

Carlie nodded then grabbed up her things and went into the house. She wasn't surprised to find that no one was home. Her family sometimes went out after mass on Sundays. Sometimes they went to Tia Maria's house or sometimes just to McDonald's where Miguel and Pedro could run themselves silly in the play area.

Carlie began putting her new school clothes away. And while she was glad that she was going to get to wear what she wanted this year, she felt like it had lost some of its appeal too. In some ways she would rather be stuck in her girly dresses and long, curly hair than to have been a part of Chelsea's sort of shopping experience.

She pulled out the blue top from the Gap bag and there — folded right into it — was that beaded blue necklace. The one that she had insisted Chelsea take back. She must've sneaked in while Carlie was asleep. No matter, she didn't have to keep it. She dropped it into her wastebasket and continued to hang up her new clothes.

After she got done, she went outside and watered her flowers. But even their bright cheery faces didn't make her feel any better. Finally, she decided to head over to the Rainbow Bus to see if any of her friends were around.

"Hey, Carlie," said Morgan as they met on the trail. "You're back from the big shopping trip. How did it go?"

And then, without any warning, Carlie began to cry. She was sobbing like a four-year-old, and she was totally embarrassed. She had no idea why she was acting like this, and she was glad that Morgan was the only one there to see it.

Morgan hugged her, just letting her cry until the tears were gone.

"Want to go down to the beach?" asked Morgan.

Carlie nodded. She really didn't want Amy or Emily to see her like this.

"What's wrong?" Morgan asked gently as they walked through the dunes.

"If you promise not to tell, I'll tell you," said Carlie.

"You can trust me."

Somehow Carlie knew she could. And so, as they walked, she told Morgan the whole story, even the part about hearing Chelsea's mom talking to her friend. "I don't know why I feel so bad about everything," she said finally. "It almost sounds kind of silly now."

"It's not silly," Morgan assured her. "I can understand how it would be upsetting to be with a friend who shoplifts. And then hearing Mrs. Landers say those things. And being away from home. I would be upset too, Carlie."

"You would?" Somehow Carlie found this hard to believe.

"Yep. I would."

"But you never seem to get upset, Morgan."

Morgan laughed. "Oh, yes I do."

"Well, somehow you handle it."

"It's not me," said Morgan.

"Huh?"

"It's Jesus in me," she explained. "When I get upset over something, I go to Jesus. I tell him what's hurting inside of me. And Jesus makes me feel better."

"Really? You just talk to him like that?"

"Yep. And he understands, Carlie. Because Jesus went through everything while he was here on earth. He knows how it feels to be picked on or disliked or even beaten ... and killed."

Carlie nodded. "I guess I never thought of it like that."

"Well, you should think about it," said Morgan. "I don't know what I'd do if I couldn't take all my troubles to Jesus."

"Do you think Amy or Emily are at the bus now?"

Morgan nodded. "Yeah, maybe we should get back."

"I will think about what you told me, Morgan."

"Good." Morgan laughed now. "Not that I'm trying to get you *saved*. Remember what Chelsea said the other day? The fact is only Jesus can save people. But I don't mind telling someone about how Jesus helps me get through hard times. I really don't know how people get by without him."

"I don't really want to tell Amy or Emily about any of this," said Carlie as they turned down the trail to the bus.

"Like I said ... you can trust me."

"Thanks."

"By the way, great haircut!" Morgan grinned. "You look very chic!"

Emily and Amy liked the haircut too. And both of them seemed genuinely happy to see her.

"You're getting so sophisticated," said Amy, pointing to Carlie's new top. "You might think you're too cool to hang with us anymore."

"Ha!" said Carlie. "Don't worry about that."

"So what about Chelsea?" asked Amy. "Are we going to invite her to join our club? We never really talked about it on Friday."

"What do you think, Carlie?" asked Morgan.

"I don't know … "

"Why?" said Amy. "Are you going to keep her to yourself?"

"No, that's not it … "

"Well, I think we should ask her to join," insisted Amy. "I think we need someone like her to class this place up a little."

Carlie felt the need to bite her tongue.

"Yeah," said Emily. "Maybe we should invite her." She held up her wrist with the bracelet. "That would be the loving thing to do."

"She might not want to join," said Carlie.

"Or do you mean you might not want to ask her?" said Amy with a suspicious look.

Carlie looked at Amy now. "Maybe you should ask her, Amy. If you're so certain that she'd like to join." But as soon as she said it, she regretted it.

"Okay," said Amy. "Maybe I will."

Carlie glanced over at Morgan, hoping she might say something to straighten this mess out. But she didn't. Instead she just smiled at Carlie and asked if they'd like to have a beading day next week.

Carlie still felt frustrated and confused when she went home. She wished she'd never met Chelsea Landers. But even more, she wished she'd never introduced her friends to Chelsea Landers. It's like Amy was not going to let it go.

"You're home," said Mom as Carlie came in the door. "I didn't hear a car."

Carlie told her she'd been home for a while, then Mom suddenly exclaimed over her hair. "Oh, it's very pretty, mija! I'm surprised to say that I like it."

Carlie was relieved. And then, since her brothers were napping, she offered to show her mom her things. But she could tell that her mom's enthusiasm wasn't totally sincere. Still, she was trying to be a good sport.

"Oh, oh," said Mom, stooping down by the waste-basket. "You must've dropped this, Carlotta. Oh, it's so pretty. Let me see it on you."

For her mother's sake, Carlie tried on the necklace. "Chelsea gave it to me," she said in a flat tone, holding up the blue top that it went with.

"Very nice." Mom nodded with approval. "You are turning into a lovely young lady, Carlotta. I'm proud of you."

Carlie wondered how proud Mom would be if she knew the truth. How would she feel to know that the necklace around her neck right now was stolen property? Carlie wished she could remember the name of the shop where Chelsea had shoplifted, but she'd been too shocked at the time to even notice. She wished she could put the stupid thing in an envelope and return it with an apology. Instead, she tucked it into her top drawer, determined to get rid of it when Mom wasn't looking.

The next few days passed uneventfully. Chelsea called several times, but Carlie was either babysitting her brothers or she made up an excuse not to see her.

Finally on Thursday, Chelsea sounded totally fed up. "Look, if you don't want to be my friend anymore, you should just say so."

Carlie was so tempted to say so, but instead she said, "I've just been really busy."

"Well, Amy hasn't been busy," snapped Chelsea. "She's called me twice this week. And today she called and invited me to come over there and hang with you guys tomorrow."

"Oh..."

"But I'm not going to come, Carlie. Not if you don't want me to come."

"It's not that …"

"What is it then?"

"I don't know …"

"Look, I told you I'm sorry for stealing those necklaces. Can't you get over it?"

"It just makes me feel bad."

"Do you still have yours?"

"Well, yes, but I —"

"Sure, you feel bad, but you kept it. What's up with that?"

"I tried to throw it away, but my mom found it. I was going to throw it away when she wasn't around. I guess I forgot. I wish I knew the name of the shop where you stole them from. I'd send it back."

"Would that make you feel better?" she asked hopefully. "If I sent them all back?"

"Yes!" Carlie felt hopeful. "It would."

"Okay, that's what I'll do then."

"You will?"

"Yes. If it will make you forget about it. I will."

So they agreed, Chelsea would come over on Friday. She would bring the stolen goods and an envelope and they would write an apology letter and send them back. Carlie hoped that would put an end to this thing, once and for all.

As planned, Chelsea came over, and they wrote a letter and took the package to town to mail from the post office. But even when they were all done, Carlie still felt badly.

"What's wrong with you?" demanded Chelsea as they went back into the trailer park.

"I don't know."

"What do you want from me? Would you be happier if I was caught and sentenced to prison or something?"

"No, that's silly. I don't know why—"

Just then Amy called out from her front porch, running out to join them. "Morgan and Emily are already at the clubhouse. We were going to head down to the beach for a while. You know there are only three days of summer vacation left. You guys coming?"

Chelsea glanced at Carlie. "Are we?"

"Sure," said Carlie without much enthusiasm. "Why not?"

Once again, Carlie loaned Chelsea her favorite swimsuit, and the two of them set off to find the others. Soon they were all down on the beach parked out at their favorite spot and just soaking up the sun. Today, Chelsea had brought her iPod in her purse and she turned on the little speaker so they had music. But for some reason the sound of the tunes only made Carlie feel worse. She closed her eyes and told herself to get over this thing—this whatever it was. Nobody wanted to hang with a girl as gloomy as she was getting to be. What was wrong with her anyway?

She listened to the other girls talking, and it seemed like Chelsea was actually trying to get along with everyone for a change. Oddly enough, it was Carlie who felt like she'd like to jump on someone. Like Amy, who was going on and on about how she was going to try out for cheerleading as soon as school started.

"That's crazy," said Carlie, sitting up. "Why would you have a chance at being a cheerleader? And why would you even want to anyway?"

Amy blinked at her. "Why not?"

"Because it's stupid."

"Sounds like somebody got up on the wrong side of bed today," teased Emily.

"I'm going for a swim," said Carlie, jumping to her feet and taking off toward the ocean.

"I'm coming too," called Chelsea.

Carlie ignored her. Mostly she just wanted to be alone. She ran past the low waves out to where the water came to her waist. As usual, it was cold, but she didn't care. She dove in and began to swim. She swam for a while, not even bothering to look back, not caring whether Chelsea was trying to catch up to her or not. Carlie was a good swimmer. She'd even considered going out for swim team, but then they had moved. Finally, she was starting to get tired, and she turned around and looked back.

Chelsea was about twenty yards behind her, waving frantically. "Come back!" she yelled, "you're going too far!"

Carlie was surprised to see how far she was from shore. Tired and cold, she began to swim back. But as she swam she noticed she didn't seem to be getting very far. And that's when she remembered the tide. Her dad had warned her many times about the tides. He'd told her not to swim too far out on certain days — that she could get caught in the tide and be pulled out to sea.

chapter twelve

"Go back!" Carlie yelled at Chelsea. "Don't come out any farther."

"No," said Chelsea. "I'll swim back with you."

"No!" screamed Carlie. "Go back, we're getting caught in the tide!"

But Chelsea stubbornly swam toward her, not turning around until they were both swimming side by side, both trying to get back to the shore.

"You should've turned back," panted Carlie as she paddled hard. "That was stupid."

"That's my middle name," said Chelsea.

"You shouldn't have wasted your energy."

"Just swim," said Chelsea.

So they swam and they swam, but they didn't seem to be getting any closer to the shore. If anything, it seemed they were steadily going backwards, getting sucked out into the enormous ocean. Carlie tried to see if her friends had noticed they were missing, but she couldn't even see the beach from out there.

"I'm tired," panted Chelsea. Her eyes were red and full of fear now. "What if we can't get back?"

"Just tread water," said Carlie breathlessly. "Try to save strength."

They stopped swimming and simply treaded water, trying to keep their heads above the occasional waves that splashed. Carlie could tell they were steadily moving farther from shore. She felt desperate now. And totally helpless. How could she have been so stupid?

"What're we going to do?" cried Chelsea.

Then Carlie suddenly remembered what Morgan had said about taking her problems to Jesus. "Pray!" screamed Carlie. "We're gonna pray!"

"I don't know how."

"Dear Jesus," cried Carlie. "Please, help us! Please, please, help us! Morgan said you could. Please, help us."

Then Chelsea started to pray in a similar way. For several minutes, both girls were crying and praying so hard that they didn't notice the orange and white helicopter hovering over them.

"Look!" screamed Carlie, pointing to a life raft that was slowly being lowered down into the ocean.

Soon they were both pulled onto the raft and wrapped in blankets. It wasn't long before a coast guard cutter came along and picked them up. They were given hot tea to drink as they were transported into Boscoe Bay. The cutter docked and a small crowd of people hurried over.

"You girls got caught in a rip tide," one of the sailors explained as he helped them down the ramp. "It's lucky you're all right."

"Chelsea!" screamed Mrs. Landers, running over to her daughter.

Soon there were people all around them. Carlie was surprised to see that her mom and two little brothers were there, as well as Morgan, Emily, Amy, and even Morgan's grandmother. Carlie ran over to them and threw her arms around her mother and brothers.

"We were so scared, mija!" cried her mom as she held her tightly in her arms. "We thought you had drowned."

"How did you know we were in trouble?" asked Carlie.

"Your friends," explained Mom between sobs. "Amy used her phone to call 9-1-1. And then she called us. We saw them pick you up, and then we drove over here."

"It was a rip tide," explained Carlie. "It just kept taking us out."

"I know," said Mom. "The coast guard man told us. No more swimming in the ocean for you!"

Carlie turned to Morgan now. "We prayed," she told her. "We really prayed hard out there, Morgan! We both cried out to Jesus to help us."

Morgan hugged her. "And he answered, didn't he?"

Carlie nodded happily.

"We were praying for you too," said Emily with tears in her eyes. "We thought for sure you guys were goners."

"I'm glad you're okay," said Amy, hugging her too. "Thanks for calling for help."

Now Chelsea and her mom came over to join them. But it looked like Mrs. Landers was seriously angry. "I just told Chelsea, and now I'm telling you too, Carlie. She is not allowed to come to your house anymore! And no more swimming in the ocean — ever! That may be okay for some people, but not my daughter! You should be ashamed of yourself!"

"Mom!" said Chelsea. "It wasn't her fault."

"Come on," said Mrs. Landers, jerking her by the arm. "You're going home right now!"

Chelsea made the shape of a phone with her hand, mouthing, "I'll call you." And Carlie just waved.

Carlie wasn't sure if it was the near-death experience or what, but as her mom drove her home — and despite the shrill voices of her brothers — she felt strangely calm and peaceful. Better than she'd felt in days.

After she got home she took a nice, hot shower and got dressed. She felt tired, but happy. And after assuring Mom that she was perfectly fine and not about to catch pneumonia, she went outside in search of her friends. She found Morgan and Emily at the clubhouse. Amy had gone to the restaurant to work.

"It's Labor Day weekend," Morgan reminded her. "They're really busy."

Carlie sank into the plush couch and let out a big sigh. "Wow."

"This was quite a day," said Morgan as she strung a bright purple bead. She and Emily were finishing up some beading projects that they'd been working on during the past week.

Carlie nodded. "Uh-huh."

"Too bad about Chelsea's mom today," said Morgan.

"Yeah," said Emily. "That seemed a little over the top."

"She'll probably get over it," said Carlie.

"You said you and Chelsea were both praying out there today?" said Morgan as she adjusted her glasses and peered curiously at Carlie.

"Yep. We both were praying."

"Cool."

Carlie got up and went to sit next to Emily at the little table. She looked across at Morgan. "I was praying to Jesus," she said, "just like you told me. And like you told me, he answered."

"Yeah?"

"But I've been wondering why he should answer me ... I mean, I pray in church, but not like you, Morgan. Not like God is really listening. I just say the words."

"He was listening," said Morgan.

"Really?"

"You should invite him into your heart," said Emily suddenly. "Like I did a couple months ago. It makes such a difference, Carlie. It'll change you completely."

Carlie considered this. "Yeah, I think you're right."

"So do you want to?" asked Emily eagerly.

"Yeah."

Both Morgan and Emily were grinning now. "You want to pray with us?" asked Morgan. "We can help you to ask Jesus into your heart."

"Okay."

So Morgan and Emily both led Carlie in a simple little prayer. And when they were done, Carlie knew that it was real—she knew that Jesus was living inside her.

"Thanks for praying with me," she told her friends.

"Welcome to the *real* club," said Morgan with a big smile.

"You know," said Carlie with fresh realization. "I think that's what I'd been wanting these past few days. It's like I was so unhappy, and I was looking for something that I just couldn't find. And I kept feeling more and more miserable and I thought it was all about Chelsea, but really it was all about me. I wanted Jesus close to me—and now I have him!"

She hugged her friends. "Thank you so much!"

"What about Chelsea?" asked Emily. "Do we want to invite her to join our club?"

Carlie considered this and to her surprise she felt totally different than she had earlier today. "You know, if we're all okay with it, I think that'd be good. I mean, I can assure you Chelsea has her faults. But then so does everyone." Carlie held up her bracelet. "And if we really mean what these stand for … well, maybe we should invite Chelsea to be part of this too."

"I'm okay with it," said Emily.

"Me too," agreed Morgan. "And we know Amy wants her to join."

"I guess it will depend on her mom," said Carlie. "She seemed pretty mad today."

"Like you said, she'll probably get over it," said Morgan. "Maybe give her a few days to cool off. In the meantime, I better make another bracelet," said Morgan. "Just in case."

To Carlie's relief, Mrs. Landers cooled off by the end of the day. "My mom said to tell you she's sorry," said Chelsea when she called her that evening. "She was upset and worried and it seems that maybe she has poor impulse control too."

Carlie chuckled. "Well, I'm glad she's over it."

"I feel like it was partly my fault that you swam so far out," said Chelsea. "I mean, I knew you were still pretty mad at me — that's why I swam out there."

So Carlie told her that had only been a small part of the problem. "I think I was more mad at myself than anything," she admitted. "It's kind of like I had allowed myself to be swept away with you and your life and your mom and stuff ... kind of like getting swept away by the tide. But somewhere inside of myself, I knew it was wrong. I knew I needed something more."

"Oh ..."

"And when I was out there with you today, and I was praying ... well, I got the feeling that I was close to it. And then afterwards, I had this amazing sense of peace, like I wasn't getting swept away anymore."

"Really?"

"Yeah. And then I invited Jesus into my heart." She laughed. "And so now I'm a Christian. You might not even want to be friends with me anymore."

Chelsea didn't say anything.

"Sorry," said Carlie. "I didn't mean to make you feel bad. It's just that I know how you feel about Christians. And now that I'm one ..."

"That's not it."

"What then?"

"I guess I just feel left out again."

"Well, no one's stopping you from becoming a Christian."

"I know ..."

"Well, anyway," said Carlie. "That's up to you. But I am supposed to ask you whether or not you want to join our club."

"Really? You guys are asking me to join?" And for the first time since Carlie had met Chelsea, she thought she really sounded happy.

"Yeah. Everyone agrees."

"All right!"

So it was that on Labor Day the five girls all met at the Rainbow Bus and Chelsea was officially welcomed into the club and presented with her own bracelet.

"Wow," she said as Morgan tied the rainbow bracelet onto her wrist. "This is so cool."

The girls took turns hugging her, and when they stopped, Chelsea actually had tears in her eyes. "Thanks," she told them. "And I'm sorry I was so mean sometimes … and I have to warn you that I can be like that … I mean, just ask Carlie … I sometimes say and do some really stupid things."

"It's okay," said Emily. "We've all got our problems."

"Yeah," said Amy. "We're pretty cool, but none of us are perfect."

They laughed.

Chelsea examined her bracelet. "Okay, now are you going to tell me what these letters stand for?"

"Love your neighbor as yourself," they all chanted together.

Chelsea considered this then nodded. "That's cool."

"It's the one rule of our club," said Morgan.

"The rule of the rainbow," added Emily with a grin.

"Rainbows rule!" said Carlie happily. She looked around at her four friends and for the first time felt like maybe she could do just that — with Jesus' help anyway. Maybe it really was possible to love others like that!

Take Charge

chapter one

"Did you guys hear the latest news?" asked Amy as soon as she entered the clubhouse, an old parked bus the girls had fixed up this past summer, to find her four friends already there and waiting for her.

"You mean that Amy Ngo is actually late for the first time in her life?" teased Carlie as she pointed to her watch.

"I'm sorry," she told them. "My mother and I were having … uh … a little discussion."

"Don't you mean more like an argument?" asked Morgan. Then she winked at Amy. "Sorry, but I couldn't help overhearing you guys on my way over here. Man, I had no idea your sweet little mom could yell like that."

Amy rolled her eyes. "Yes, well, my mother seems to have gotten the idea that I'm spoiled."

"Goodness," said Emily with wide blue eyes. "Where would she get an idea like that?" The other girls laughed.

"Thanks a lot!" Amy frowned at the four of them.

"Hey," said Chelsea, "don't feel too bad. These guys think I'm spoiled too. You're in good company."

Amy sank down into the couch next to Chelsea, folding her arms across her chest. "Fine," she snapped.

"Maybe we are both a little bit spoiled. But I'm a hard worker too!"

"I know you are," said Morgan in a kind voice. "We all know you are."

"Now, what's the news, Amy?" asked Emily. "What did you want to tell us?"

"You guys didn't hear what happened last night?" She looked hopefully at her four friends. She loved being the person who knew something that the others hadn't heard yet. Of course, she didn't like the title that often went with it. All during grade school she had suffered being called Miss Ngo It All. But since starting seventh grade, she'd been trying to avoid that label.

"No, Amy," said Carlie. "Spill the beans!"

"Well, you know last night was the first football game at Boscoe Bay High, and they weren't supposed to win —"

"But they beat the pants off of Wedgeport," interrupted Emily. "That's old news, Amy. My brother actually took me to the game, and it was a —"

"That's *not* my news," said Amy. She scowled at Emily.

"Okay then," said Morgan. "What is it?"

"According to today's newspaper, it happened after the game last night. A bunch of vandals from Wedgeport High attacked the city park and made a total mess of it."

"McPhearson Park?" asked Morgan sadly.

"Yes. They actually drove their four-wheel-drive vehicles into the park and pulled down the swings and lampposts and knocked over trees and everything. The grass was totally torn up from their tires. The photo in the newspaper made it look like a hurricane had hit. I would've brought it, but my dad was still reading the editorials."

"That's too bad," said Emily. "That was such a pretty park."

"I know …" Amy sighed. "I used to play there all the time when I was a little girl. I have so many happy memories of it … and now it looks like a war zone."

"Well, I'm sure they will fix it up and it —"

"No," said Amy quickly. "That's just the problem. It sounds like there are no funds in the city budget to cover the cost of the repairs. And even worse than that, a lot of the businesses in town, including my very own parents, have wanted to get rid of the park for several years now."

"Get rid of it?" Morgan adjusted her glasses and peered curiously at Amy. "Why would anyone want that?"

"For a stupid parking lot!" said Amy. "In fact, that's what started my argument with my mom this morning."

"Why does Boscoe Bay need a parking lot?" asked Emily.

"I know why," said Chelsea. "In fact, my dad would agree with Amy's parents on this. He says there's no place to park in town, and all the tourist business is going down to the waterfront."

"That's because the waterfront is cool," said Morgan.

"Of course *you'd* say that," said Amy. "Your mom's shop is there."

"Lots of people think the waterfront is cool," protested Emily.

"Yeah, but they might not think it was so cool if there was no place to park down there," pointed out Chelsea.

"I'd still go there," said Carlie. "Even if I had to walk a mile and a—"

"But you're not a grown-up with a—"

"Okay, *okay!*" said Morgan, holding up both hands and starting to wear her presidential expression. "That is *not* what this meeting is about." Then she pointed to her colorful beaded bracelet. "Rainbows rule, you guys. *Remember.*"

"Sorry," said Amy, although she still felt angry about what was going on in town. But she did know the meaning of the bracelet—even if she didn't fully get the religious connection, she was well aware that the letters on the beads, LYNAY, meant to *love your neighbor as yourself,* which meant the girls needed to respect one another. And for now it meant that Amy needed to close her mouth.

"Anyway," continued Morgan. "As you know, this is our first official meeting since school started. And the main item on our agenda today is to discuss a new project."

Emily took out a notepad. "I'm ready."

"Okay," said Morgan. "I'm sure you guys remember how we decided at our last meeting that it helps us to stay together as a group when we're all working toward the same thing. It doesn't have to be a big thing, especially since school has started. But we do need something to keep us focused and united as a group ... " She looked at the girls and sort of laughed. "Because, as you can see, it's easy to get going in all kinds of different directions ... and before you know it, we're in a big old fight."

"And then it's no fun being in a club together," said Emily.

"That's right," said Morgan. "So we're open to suggestions now. Anyone?"

The bus grew quiet for a long moment.

"Okay, for Chelsea's benefit, since she's new, I'll go over a bit of our history," said Morgan. "Maybe that will get things rolling. Let's see ... we sort of became friends last spring because of the bullies."

"The bullies?" said Chelsea.

So Carlie quickly retold the story of how Derrick Smith and his gang of thugs had picked on them and helped to unite them as friends.

"But Derrick is in juvenile detention now," said Emily.

"And his old friends have changed their ways," added Morgan.

"In fact," said Carlie, "I think Jeff Sanders has a big crush on Emily."

"Does not," said Emily.

"Does so," said Carlie.

"You guys!" yelled Morgan.

"Sorry." Emily giggled.

"Back to our history." Morgan peered at Emily. "Are you getting this down, Ms. Secretary?"

"Oh, yeah." Emily got busy writing again.

"Anyway, after we became friends, we did a major cleanup on the trailer park," continued Morgan. "We knew it looked pretty shabby and that it was probably one of the reasons we were being teased. So we really cleaned it up."

"And then Mr. Greeley, the owner of the trailer park, gave us the bus," said Carlie. "It had been sitting here empty for about ten years."

"It was pretty dirty and messy. We fixed it up," added Amy.

"And then there was the sand-castle-building contest," said Emily. She told Chelsea how they made SpongeBob SquarePants.

"But Derrick Smith destroyed it," said Amy.

"And we still won the People's Choice Award," finished off Carlie.

"So what's next?" asked Chelsea.

"That's what we need to decide," said Morgan. "That's why—"

"I know!" said Amy suddenly. *"I know!"*

"Uh-oh," said Carlie. "Miss Ngo It All has just arrived."

Amy scowled at Carlie.

"Sorry," muttered Carlie.

"Do you have an idea, Amy?" asked Morgan.

Amy frowned. "Not if I'm going to be teased."

"I said I was sorry," said Carlie.

"Okay …" Amy looked at the other four girls in the bus. She wasn't sure they'd be up for this or even able to pull it off, but it was worth a shot. "How about if we help fix up McPhearson Park?"

The girls got quiet again so Amy went on. "I used to spend a lot of time there. When my family was busy at the restaurant and I was too little to help, I'd go and swing on the swings … or ride the merry-go-round. I can't believe that it could turn into a big, ugly cement parking lot."

Morgan nodded. "Yes, that does seem wrong."

"But fixing up a park sounds like a huge project," said Chelsea. "And we're, like, *five* girls."

"We got the trailer park fixed up," Emily reminded her.

"And we wouldn't have to do it all ourselves," said Morgan. "We could rally support from the community, get the ball rolling."

"Or start a big old war," said Chelsea. "I mean, with people like my dad and Amy's parents — the ones who want a parking lot — it could get ugly."

"But what about the kids in this town?" said Amy. "The park is for them. Shouldn't we stand up for the kids?"

"That's right," said Morgan. "And it might help that we're kids too. I mean, older kids, obviously, but we're still young enough that grown-ups might feel guilty to think they're taking away our park."

"I like this idea," said Carlie. "And maybe we could get more permits to dig plants from the woods. I'm sure my dad would take us up there again."

"And maybe we could do a fund-raiser," said Chelsea. "My old school used to do fund-raisers every year. My mom was usually the head of the committee."

"Are you getting all this down, Emily?" asked Morgan.

"Writing as fast as I can," she said.

"I think we should check it out for ourselves," said Morgan suddenly. "You guys wanna walk to town and take a look at McPhearson Park?"

So it was decided that they would take a field trip. As they walked toward town, Amy felt like crossing her fingers. She so wanted this to work.

"Oh, my!" said Morgan when the girls turned the corner and came into sight of the park.

"What a total wreck!" said Emily.

Tears filled Amy's eyes as she looked at the ruined park with yellow police tape surrounding it like a crime scene, which it was. "This is so wrong!" she said, stamping her foot.

"Where would we even begin?" asked Chelsea. "I mean, the whole place seems ruined."

"We'd begin by getting support from the community," declared Amy. "And the sooner the better."

"So are we in?" asked Morgan. "Can I see a quick show of hands here? Who is in favor of saving McPhearson Park?"

They all raised their hands and said "Aye."

"So be it," said Morgan.

Amy looked across the street to where her parents' restaurant, Asian Garden, was located. She thought she spied her mother looking out the window toward the vandalized park. And, okay, maybe she was imagining things now, but she thought she saw her mother rubbing her hands together in happy anticipation of what might soon be a cement parking lot!

Not if I can help it, thought Amy.

chapter two

On Sunday afternoon the girls met at the bus to begin planning their strategy for cleaning up McPhearson Park.

"I've done some research," said Amy as soon as their meeting began. She opened the notebook that she'd been making notes in since yesterday.

"Oh, no," Carlie groaned. "This is feeling like school."

"It's just a little historical background," said Amy, trying not to sound offended. "I'll try to keep it short, okay?"

"Go ahead," said Morgan. "It might be interesting."

Amy cleared her throat. "Boscoe Bay was discovered by a sea captain named Henry McPhearson in 1859. He named the bay in honor of his fiancée, Amelia Boscoe, whom he soon married. About a dozen years later, the couple settled here and eventually founded the town of Boscoe Bay in 1880. And in 1911, Captain McPhearson died, and his family purchased a parcel of land in the center of town, which they dedicated to his memory and turned into a park."

"That's nice," said Carlie. "But what's your point, Amy?"

Amy forced a smile. "Just be patient, Carlie. Who knows, maybe you'll actually learn something."

Emily held back a laugh.

"The good news is that the city doesn't actually own the park," said Amy. "So they don't have control over the land, and it can't be turned into a parking lot."

"So it can remain a park forever?" asked Morgan.

Amy frowned. "Well, according to my online research and a phone call to the mayor —"

"You *called* the mayor?" said Carlie.

Amy nodded. "Why not? Anyway, he told me that the city has been trying to get control of the land for a few years now, but the McPhearson family still owns it, and it seems they're unwilling to sell."

"Good for them," said Carlie. Then she frowned. "But I still don't get your point."

"Yeah, and what's the bad news?" asked Morgan.

"The bad news is that we can't touch the park or do a thing to help it without getting permission from the family first."

"What's so bad about that?"

"There's only one member of the family still living in town," she told them.

"And?" persisted Morgan.

"And the mayor said she's a crazy old spinster woman named Viola McPhearson who won't talk to anyone — not even the mayor."

"Oh…" Morgan frowned. "So what happens to the park?"

"The mayor said that the city attorney will send Miss McPhearson a letter informing her that she has thirty days to make repairs to the park."

"What if she doesn't do anything?" asked Morgan.

"Then the property will be confiscated by the city."

"And turned into a parking lot?" asked Emily.

Amy shrugged. "The mayor didn't admit it, but I'm sure that's the plan."

"What do we do now?" asked Carlie.

"Do you think we could talk to the old lady?" asked Morgan.

"The mayor said she's crazy and has been known to greet unexpected visitors with a shotgun."

"Whoa." Chelsea shook her head. "That sounds a little scary."

"Yeah." Amy sat down at the table and sighed.

"Maybe we could call her first," said Morgan. "Explain who we are and how we want to help save her family's park."

"I looked in the phone book," said Amy, "and even called information… There's no listing for Viola McPhearson, or any other McPhearsons in Boscoe Bay."

"So maybe there's nothing we can do," said Morgan.

"Maybe ..." said Amy. "But it's hard to let it go. It just seems so wrong to allow it to become a parking lot." She slammed her fist down onto the table. "Kids need trees and swings and a place to go where they can just play and be kids." She felt tears burning in her eyes again. Why was this thing with the park making her so upset?

Morgan put her hand on Amy's shoulder. "We agree with you, Amy. But it doesn't seem like there's anything we can do about it."

Amy looked up suddenly as an idea hit her. "Okay, maybe we can't do anything about the crazy lady. But we can try to influence the city."

"How?" asked Emily, looking up from her note taking.

"We'll all write letters to the editor. My dad is always reading them, and I think a lot of other people read them. We'll start a Save the Park campaign that's directed at the city."

"Why not?" said Morgan. "Maybe we can make them see how important it is for Boscoe Bay to keep the park."

"Right," said Emily. "I'd be glad to write a letter."

Carlie groaned. "See, this *is* becoming like schoolwork. And I hate to write. Which reminds me, I have a book report due in English tomorrow. I should probably go work on it."

"Well, we don't all have to write at once," said Emily. "I'll make sure I get a letter out today, then maybe it'll get printed in Tuesday's paper. But we can stagger our letters to make sure there's one in each edition." She pointed to Carlie. "And I'll help you write a letter, Carlie."

Carlie smiled. "Will you help me write a book report too?"

"Sure," said Emily.

"And will you read the book for me?" asked Carlie.

"Carlie!" scolded Emily. "You can't expect me to do everything for you."

The girls laughed and Emily began working on her letter.

"I'm going to have to go," said Amy, glancing at her watch. "I have to work at the restaurant this afternoon. My sister An has a date."

"An has a date?" echoed Morgan. "Is it serious?"

Amy laughed. "Let's hope it's serious for An. Good grief, my older sister, Ly, is going to be thirty in December, and I don't think she'll ever get married."

"I don't get that," said Emily. "How is it that your sisters and your brother are all still single?"

Amy shrugged as she paused by the door. "I guess it's because my parents insisted on them working in the restaurant to help pay for their education. And between college and work, there's not much time left for a love life." She didn't mention that her parents insisted that each of her siblings date and marry only someone from their homeland. And there weren't too many Vietnamese people around to choose from.

"See you guys later," she called as she left. She wished she could stay and hang with her friends a little longer. But after the fight with her mother earlier, she knew she better not press her luck. Not only that, but her parents' mood would only get worse when they discovered that An was going out with a guy who was NOT Vietnamese — although Amy had no plans to tell them.

She walked back to the trailer park, going directly to the mobile home that was inhabited by her three siblings. She tried not to envy them their independence — after all, they were all in their twenties. It was so much more relaxed and fun in their house.

"Hey, squirt," said her brother, Tu'. "You ready to head out to the salt mines?"

She nodded. "Yeah, can't wait."

"Thanks for filling in for me tonight," called An. "I owe you one, Amy."

"Are you going to drop by the restaurant later on tonight and introduce the parents to your new beau?" asked Tu'.

An laughed. "Yeah, right."

"Let's go," said Tu', opening the door for her. "Ly will probably yell at us if we're late."

Amy nodded. Ly was the slave driver among her three siblings. Maybe it was because she was the oldest, but Amy couldn't help but think it was because Ly was unhappy. Ly was short and stocky and not very pretty. But An was taller and willowy and pretty. Amy hoped that she would grow up to look like An, not only in appearance — although that was important enough to Amy — but also in disposition. Between the two sisters, An was by far the most kindhearted. If Amy ever needed anything, she always went to An first.

Amy told Tu' a little about the research she'd done on McPhearson Park for their Save the Park campaign.

He laughed. "Well, the parents are not going to like that, Amy."

She smiled. "I know. But I'm an independent person, Tu'. I can think for myself."

He laughed even harder now. "Well, it's about time. But don't forget that we've helped to pave that road for you. Even today," he continued. "An is really pushing it to go out with this guy."

"Are you against it too?" asked Amy.

He shook his head. "Not at all. I met him the other night, and he seems really nice. Did An tell you that he finished med school last spring and recently started interning at a hospital in Newport?"

"No," said Amy. "You'd think *that* would impress Mom and Dad."

He sighed. "You'd think."

"How about you, Tu'?" she asked. "Don't you ever want to date?"

He gave her a sideways glance. "You don't know everything about me, Amy Ngo."

"Meaning?"

"Meaning, if I could trust you, I'd answer that."

"*You can trust me, Tu'.*"

He grinned. "Well, did it ever occur to you that maybe I do date?"

"You do?"

He nodded. "I just don't go around telling the parents about it."

"Oh…"

"Not that I'm saying we should be sneaky. But I am twenty-six and old enough to make my own decisions. I just don't like telling the parents because I know it'll only cause trouble."

"So I'm guessing you're not dating nice Asian girls then?"

He chuckled. "They're nice girls. Just not Asian." He glanced nervously at her. "But you won't tell, will you?"

"My lips are sealed."

"Thanks."

They were at the restaurant now, parking in the small gravel lot out back. Tu' locked the car, and they went in through the back door.

"It's about time," said Ly, tossing a towel at Amy. "Get to work on those pans, will you?" She glared at Tu'. "You were supposed to be here an hour ago."

He shrugged as he glanced out the little window to the dining room. "It's okay, Ly. There's hardly anyone out there anyway."

She muttered something to him in Vietnamese and returned to washing cabbage. Amy started drying pans and placing them on the shelves, listening as her parents talked to Ly and Tu' in Vietnamese and wishing they'd work harder on their English skills. Her father's English was a whole lot better than her mother's, but it could use some serious work. Amy had offered to help them — lots of times — but they were either too busy or too tired or just not interested. She had just about given up on them entirely.

She had just returned the last pot to its shelf when she heard her mother telling Ly that she had found a new kitchen helper — part-time only — and that Ly would be helping Amy wait tables tonight if it got busy.

"Why can't your new helper wait tables?" asked Ly in English. Ly didn't like being out in the public. She preferred the kitchen, and no one could argue that anyone was better than her — especially when it came to the knives. Then her mother explained — in Vietnamese — that the new helper didn't speak very good English.

Amy tried not to laugh.

"Who is this person anyway?" demanded Ly.

Her mother explained that the girl was the daughter
of a friend, that they had recently emigrated here from
Thailand, but that they were originally from Vietnam. And
then, in a hushed tone, she told Ly that this girl would be a
perfect match for Tu'.

Ly laughed loudly, and Amy glanced over to where
Tu' was helping Dad with something on the computer in
the little office just off of the kitchen. He obviously hadn't
heard their mother's comment. Not that it would matter.
Sure, her mother could bring in a Vietnamese girl, but that
didn't mean Tu' had to like her. Not for the first time, Amy
thought about how strange her life must seem to her friends.

It was about five o'clock when the new employee
arrived. Amy took a quick peek at her as she filled out
some paperwork in the office. She seemed a nice enough
person, and despite what her mother had said, she seemed
to have a better grasp on English than either of Amy's
parents.

"Hello?" With her head lowered, the girl spoke
directly to Tu' when she came back into the kitchen. "Your
mother say you will show me around, please?"

"Amy!" called Tu' as he removed a large, bulky cut of
pork from the cooler. "Can you help her, please? I'm busy
here."

"Sorry," said the girl, stepping back.

"Hi," said Amy with a smile. "I'm Amy. I can show you around."

"Thank you." The girl smiled. "I'm Cara."

So Amy gave her a quick tour of the kitchen and restaurant, finally putting her to work prepping the vegetables. Not Amy's favorite task. Especially the onions, which were next. Then Amy removed her apron and went out to the restaurant to take her place acting as hostess and waitress.

For the most part, it looked as if the tables were set and ready. Amy checked on the water pitchers and straightened a few things, and before long, people began to trickle in for dinner.

As usual, Amy was polite and helpful as she seated people and filled their water glasses and took their orders. She smiled as she brought them tea and eventually fortune cookies when they were finished with their meals. But she was a little bored with the work and wondered how all her siblings had managed to stick around so long, patiently working in the restaurant while attending college at a snail's pace. She had a feeling that she would be the first one to break the tradition.

Finally, it was after eight o'clock and the restaurant was empty. Amy wished she could go home. If An were here, she knew the two of them would sneak out on the pretext that Amy had homework. But Tu' had to stay and help clean up. So Amy went to the kitchen to see how their new worker had fared.

"Want some help?" asked Amy when she found Cara rinsing pots to go into the dishwasher.

"Thank you," said Cara.

"How did it go tonight?" asked Amy as she sprayed a saucepan.

"Good, I think."

"How long have you been in town?" asked Amy.

"About a year."

"A year?" Amy was surprised. For some reason, she thought Cara had just arrived. "Where do you live?"

"On Amelia Lane," said Cara carefully, as if she was practicing her English. "Two mile from here."

"With your family?" asked Amy.

"No. My family stay in California. I come here to work. I care for a woman. I cook and clean."

"Oh." Amy nodded.

"And now sometime I come here to help in restaurant too." She smiled.

Amy figured that must have more to do with her brother, Tu', than anything else. Not that it was Amy's business, but as far as she could tell, Tu' didn't seem the least bit interested in poor Cara.

"So you live with the woman you care for?" said Amy, just trying to make small talk until they finished up the pans.

"Yes. She is strange woman. She can do things ... but she must have someone at night. She is scary."

"*Scary?*"

"Afraid."

"Oh, you mean she's scared."

"Yes. Scared. She say ghosts come to her house. But she is scary too. I call her Dragon Lady. Not so she can hear."

Amy chuckled. "Sounds interesting."

Cara smiled. "Some people say Miss McPhearson is crazy."

"*Miss McPhearson?*" said Amy eagerly. "You mean Viola McPhearson?"

Cara clapped her hand over her mouth. "Oh, dear! Do you know her? Sorry, I do not mean she is real Dragon Lady; I just —"

"No, that's okay. I mean, I don't really know her," said Amy quickly. "But I know who she is. And I would really like to meet her."

Cara frowned. "She does not like people much."

"You don't think it would be possible for me to meet her then?"

She firmly shook her head. "No."

"Maybe I could send a message to her," suggested Amy.

Cara nodded now. "Yes. I could take her a message."

So Amy ran into the office and quickly wrote a note. Using her best handwriting, she told Miss McPhearson that she had an urgent need to meet her and to discuss something of great importance because McPhearson Park was in danger of being bulldozed for a parking lot. Sure, she knew it was a long shot, but it was worth a try. She put the note into an envelope and took it back to Cara.

"I am not sure …" said Cara as she tucked the note into her purse, "that she will read it."

"That's okay," said Amy as she crossed both fingers behind her back. "But I can hope she will."

Amy knew that her friends would pray right now. But Amy had never really prayed before. And although Amy knew a lot about a lot of things, she knew next to nothing about prayer. Maybe she should ask An about it. She knew that An had become a Christian and that she went to a church in town. An had invited Amy to come with her, but her parents had made it clear that one daughter being tied up with church on Sunday morning was more than enough for their family!

chapter three

"Did you see the newspaper this morning?" Amy asked her friends as they met to walk to school together on Tuesday.

"Were our letters in it?" asked Emily hopefully.

"Yes!" exclaimed Amy.

"Both of them?" asked Morgan.

"Yes, both of them!"

"That's so cool," said Morgan. "I've got my letter all ready to go now."

"Okay, Emily," said Carlie. "You better help me get mine done too."

"Have you heard anything back from Miss McPhearson yet?" asked Morgan.

Amy shook her head. "Not a word."

"How about the girl who works for her?"

"Cara hasn't called either. And unless someone in my family gets sick or has a date, I don't think she'll be working at the restaurant much." Amy laughed. "Unless I can somehow convince my brother that he's really in love with her after all."

"Your parents actually hired her because they thought Tu' would fall for her?" said Emily.

"Like I told you," said Amy, not wanting to go into the whole story again, "they are very old-fashioned."

"Hey, don't feel bad," said Carlie. "My family is like that about some things too. According to my mom, it hasn't been that long since the people in her family arranged marriages for their children. Can you believe it?"

"Who knows?" said Emily. "Maybe it would be better for some people than letting them arrange their own marriages." She frowned. "My parents sure didn't do too well."

"And my parents never even got married," said Morgan.

"What?" Amy turned and looked at Morgan. "Are you serious?"

Suddenly Morgan seemed embarrassed. But she nodded.

"It's not that big of a deal," said Emily quickly. "Lots of people have kids without getting married."

"Not in my family," said Amy.

"Or mine," added Carlie.

"Well, I'm not saying it was a good thing," admitted Morgan. "And there are lots of times when I really wish my dad was around ... but I know my mom had her reasons. And she's not perfect, but I love her."

Amy considered this. "Whose parents *are* perfect?"

"Not mine," said Carlie.

"Not mine either," added Morgan.

"For sure not mine," said Emily.

"I used to think that Chelsea had perfect parents," said Carlie. "But after I got to know them a little better … well, I know they're not."

They turned down the street to Washington Middle School and Amy began to walk a little faster.

"Hey, what's the hurry?" asked Morgan.

"Sorry," said Amy. "Just an old habit." Amy used to take pride in being the first one at school each day. She liked helping their teacher and getting herself ready for the day. Now that they had lots of teachers and lots of classes, it didn't seem to matter so much whether she was early or not. Still, she didn't want to be late for English.

"We've got plenty of time," Carlie assured her.

"So what are we going to do about McPhearson Park?" asked Morgan. "I mean, if we can't contact Viola McPhearson — what's our next plan of action?"

"You mean besides writing letters to the editor?" said Emily.

"Yeah," said Morgan. "That's a good start and it might get some attention, but we need to do more."

"Especially if the city only gives Miss McPhearson a month to respond to their letter," added Carlie.

"That means the park could be turned into a parking lot by the middle of October," said Amy.

"Should we make a plan to start raising money?" asked Carlie.

"I think we should have a meeting after school today," said Morgan as they started up the steps to the school. "To discuss this further."

"Hey, you guys!" called Chelsea as she popped out of a white Mercedes and waved. "Wait up!"

So the four of them waited as Chelsea jogged on over.

"I saw your letters in the paper," said Chelsea breathlessly as she joined them at the top of the stairs.

"Cool, huh?" said Amy.

"Yeah." Then Chelsea frowned. "But my dad didn't like it."

"What did he say?"

"He wanted to know if I knew you guys." She giggled. "That's like my dad, you know ... so checked out. Well, Mom set him straight and then he got really grumpy. He said we should mind our own business."

"Like the park's *not* our business?" demanded Amy.

"Yeah," said Morgan. "If the park's not our business and we're kids, then whose business is it anyway?"

Chelsea laughed. "Yeah, that's kinda what I told him."

"Well, we're going to have a meeting after school," said Morgan.

"Today?" asked Chelsea.

"Yeah, why not?"

"Today's soccer tryouts."

"That's right," said Carlie. "I totally forgot!"

"Oh, why do you guys want to do that?" asked Amy. She'd never been very into sports and didn't know why her friends would want to go get all sweaty and dirty on purpose.

"Because it'll be fun," said Carlie.

"I always do soccer," said Chelsea.

"You guys should try out too," said Carlie. "Especially you, Morgan. Besides me, you're the fastest runner I know."

Morgan smiled. "Thanks. But I don't know much about soccer." She pointed to her glasses. "And it's kind of hard with these."

"You can get special sports glasses," said Chelsea. "My friend back in Minnesota had them. They look kind of dorky, but they do protect your eyes."

"Come on," urged Carlie. "You'd probably like it, if you just gave it a chance."

"I used to play soccer," said Emily in a quiet voice.

"See," said Chelsea. "You should try out too, Emily! Come on, everyone, it'll be fun."

So it was agreed — or so it seemed — they should all try out for soccer. Still, Amy wasn't so sure. She wasn't very athletic, and she didn't like looking stupid. She'd already made a fool of herself once this year when she tried out for seventh-grade cheerleading during the first week of school. *What had she been thinking?* Even though she'd learned the routine and performed it without one single mistake, she just didn't seem to have that "special something" that won the other girls spots on the small cheerleading team. Still, it had been some consolation when her friends had cheered her on and told her she was brave to try out.

At the end of the day Amy begged out. "I just don't want to," she told her friends. "I have music to practice and schoolwork to do and I sometimes help at the restaurant. I don't see how I'd have time for soccer too."

But she felt left out when she started for home after school by herself. Part of her wished that she'd gone ahead and tried out. Like Carlie had assured the others, "Don't worry, no one gets cut from seventh-grade soccer." Still, Amy felt pretty sure she might've been cut. Especially if she fell on her face like she figured she would. Instead of going directly home, she decided to go through town and stop by the restaurant. She knew that Tuesday was almond cookie day, and she figured at least she could get a good snack.

But before going into the restaurant, she stopped to look at what used to be McPhearson Park. It was still cordoned off with yellow police tape. And it looked even more dismal than when she'd seen it before. It seemed that no one really cared whether or not it was turned into a parking lot.

Determined not to cry, Amy swallowed hard against a lump that was growing in her throat. Maybe this was like so many other things to do with childhood. Maybe it was just time for her to grow up and move on.

"This used to be such a pretty park," said a voice to her left.

Amy turned to see an older woman standing by a white car. She was looking out over the devastated park and sadly shaking her head.

"Yes," said Amy. "I was just thinking that exact same thing." She walked over to the woman. "I used to play here when I was a little girl."

"So did I," said the woman. Then she laughed. "Of course that was long, long ago. But I can remember when bands would play over there." She pointed to an empty spot in the center of the park. "Oh, it's not there now, but there used to be a lovely white gazebo. And on a warm summer Sunday afternoon, they would have concerts here. Sometimes a brass band would play jazz or swing. And sometimes we would have dances in the evening. It was really grand."

"That sounds nice," said Amy. "I'm a musician too. I think it would be fun to have a concert here."

"Oh, it would be wonderful. Something for young people to do. Like when I was a girl. We had such fun here."

Suddenly Amy got this crazy wave of hope. Could it be possible that this was old Viola McPhearson standing right here before her? Could Amy have gotten that lucky?

"I don't remember seeing a gazebo here before," she told the woman, studying her closely, hoping against hope that this was the mysterious Viola.

"Of course not, dear. It was taken down long ago, back in the fifties, I believe. They thought it was dangerous. And I suppose it was falling apart some — the way old things tend to do. The city refused to pay to have it replaced. And now it's simply a memory. Although I believe there may be photographs of it somewhere. I may even have some of them myself."

"I've been doing some historical research on the park," said Amy. "I understand that it belongs to the McPhearson family."

The woman nodded. "Yes, that's right."

"I even spoke to the mayor about it," she continued.

"Really?" The woman peered curiously at Amy now. "You spoke to the mayor yourself?"

Amy nodded, standing a little taller. "He told me that a letter would be sent to Miss Viola McPhearson, asking her to take care of repairing the park within thirty days."

"And then what?"

"If she doesn't, the city will take it over. And most likely it will become a parking lot." Amy watched for the woman's reaction.

But she just made a *tsk-tsk* sound. "Well, I have a feeling that poor old Viola won't pay much heed to that letter."

"Do you *know* her?" asked Amy.

"I knew her once … long ago. She's a few years older than me. But she was a good friend of my oldest sister, Margaret, when they were in school together. Of course, Margaret's been gone a few years now. Not that she and Viola stayed in touch. Viola is a bit of a recluse." She looked at Amy. "Do you know what a recluse is, dear?"

"Of course," said Amy. "That's a person who keeps to herself."

The woman smiled. "You sound like a smart young lady."

Amy smiled back.

Now the woman extended her hand. "I'm sorry. Where are my manners? My name is Martha Watson."

"I am Amy Ngo," she told her, nodding across the street. "My family owns Asian Garden."

"Oh, yes," said the woman. "I ate there once when I was passing through town."

"You don't live here?"

"Oh, no. I haven't lived here for years. I just like to come through from time to time. Just for memory's sake."

"Oh…"

"But I'm sorry to hear you may be losing the park. It's a pity."

Amy nodded. "Yes, it is. My friends and I are going to do everything we can to save it. We're writing letters to the editor, and we plan to raise money, and we'd like to get people in town to support our cause."

"Well, it's a good cause. And if I lived in town, I'd certainly support it."

"Thanks," said Amy. "That's something."

"But not much," admitted the woman. Then she opened her purse. "How about if I give you my address," she said as she opened a little notepad and wrote something down. "And if your campaign to save the park gets off the ground, you can write to me and I'll do what I can to help."

"Thanks, Mrs. Watson," said Amy as she slipped the paper into her backpack.

"And now I think I'd like to find a place to get a cup of tea."

"We have tea," said Amy. "At the restaurant, I mean."

Mrs. Watson smiled. "Yes, I'm sure you do."

"And my mother makes almond cookies on Tuesdays," continued Amy.

"Almond cookies?" Mrs. Watson looked interested.

"Do you want to join me?" asked Amy.

Mrs. Watson nodded. "I think that I would."

Soon Amy and her new friend were seated at the restaurant. An had tossed Amy a curious look when they came in, but Amy had introduced Mrs. Watson as if it wasn't the least bit strange that she was having tea and cookies with a woman more than seven times older than her. Amy had already done the math.

"These are delicious," said Mrs. Watson as she picked up another cookie and examined it. "Your mother could probably package these and sell them."

Amy smiled. "I'll make sure to tell her that."

"And now I'm thinking …" Mrs. Watson sighed. "If Viola still lives in the family home, which I'm guessing she must, maybe it would be worthwhile to pay her a little visit."

Amy's hopes soared. "Do you think —"

"And if your parents will let you go, I could take you along with me."

"Oh, I'm sure they won't mind."

"But we may get the brush-off, Amy." Mrs. Watson studied Amy's face.

"That's okay," said Amy. "I've heard that she's not very hospitable."

Mrs. Watson laughed. "I'm afraid that may be putting it mildly."

So Amy and Mrs. Watson talked to Amy's mother — with Amy working as translator — and it was agreed that Amy could accompany the older woman to the McPhearson house. Of course, it didn't hurt matters that

Mrs. Watson wanted to buy two dozen almond cookies to take home with her.

Once again, Amy wished that she knew how to pray as Mrs. Watson drove them up the coast highway. And she was tempted to pull out her cell phone to call Morgan — via Chelsea's cell phone — and ask her to pray. But she didn't.

chapter four

After just a few minutes of driving, Mrs. Watson turned off the main highway onto Amelia Lane. Amy remembered that Cara had mentioned that name only a few days ago. She wondered if she would see Cara there today and whether Cara had given Miss McPhearson her note.

"Do you think Amelia Lane is named after Captain McPhearson's wife?" asked Amy as Mrs. Watson turned onto a long, graveled driveway with tall hedges growing up both sides. "You know he married Amelia Boscoe before founding the town."

"I think that's a very good guess," said Mrs. Watson as she parked in front of a large dark house that loomed before them like a tall shadow. It was made of charcoal-colored stone and had what Amy imagined might be a Gothic look to it.

"Wow," said Amy. "That's one spooky-looking house."

Mrs. Watson chuckled. "Yes, I remember having that same feeling long ago when I came up here with Margaret for a birthday party. I'd never seen the house up close before, and with all its turrets and leaded windows and oversized doors, well, I thought that perhaps a giant or a witch lived inside."

Amy laughed nervously as she remembered what Cara had said about the Dragon Lady. "I can see how you'd think that. Was it any less frightening once you got inside? For the party, I mean?"

"Oh, yes. It was perfectly lovely. All lit up and decorated with balloons and streamers and party things. My, they used to give some wonderful parties up here in those days. You see, Viola was an only child and, as I recall, she had everything a girl could possibly want back then. I even remember feeling slightly jealous of her … especially during the Depression when so many of us were making do with hand-me-downs and resoled shoes and whatnot. But Viola always seemed to have things that looked new and expensive." Mrs. Watson laughed as she turned off the engine. "It seems rather silly now, but I can remember feeling very disturbed about it when I was a girl. It just didn't seem fair."

"I've felt like that before," admitted Amy. In particular she was remembering how jealous she'd been the first time she'd gone to Chelsea's house. It seemed as if Chelsea had everything too. Still, Amy had tried not to show her envy. And eventually she became pretty good friends with Chelsea. But the truth was she still struggled with the green-eyed monster sometimes.

Mrs. Watson got out of the car and looked at Amy. "Are you ready for this?"

"I guess so."

"Well, as you know, we may not get past the front door."

Amy crossed her fingers as they walked up the paved path to the large and intimidating front door. It did look as if a giant or even a Dragon Lady might live here.

Mrs. Watson rang the doorbell and Amy held her breath as they waited. After a few minutes Cara opened the door, but she looked completely shocked to see them there. "Oh!" She looked from Amy to Mrs. Watson then back at Amy again, holding her hand over her mouth.

"This is Mrs. Watson," said Amy quickly. "She's an old friend of Miss McPhearson's." Then she turned to Mrs. Watson. "And this is Cara … uh, I don't know her last name, but she's a friend of my mother and works at our restaurant sometimes." She turned back to Cara, who still looked stunned.

"I've come to see Viola," said Mrs. Watson.

"Yes." Cara still looked cautious as she opened the door wider. "Uh, come in. I will go tell her." Then she led them into a large foyer with stone floors and a winding staircase that seemed to go on forever. Amy tried not to stare at everything, but she wanted to take it all in.

The ornate furniture looked as if it had come from other countries, including Asia, as had some of her own family's pieces. Although they had nothing as grand as any of this.

"I assume many of these furnishings were collected by old Captain McPhearson," said Mrs. Watson as if reading Amy's thoughts, "as he traveled about the world. Imagine the stories these pieces could tell … "

"They look very old."

Mrs. Watson nodded. "And quite valuable, I'm sure."

They stood for what seemed like a long time, and Amy worried that Mrs. Watson might be getting tired. She pointed to an upholstered bench against the wall. "Do you want to sit down?"

"That's a good idea." Mrs. Watson walked over and sat down, putting her purse in her lap. Amy sat beside her. This was so strange. She felt as if she'd just been transported to another place or was living out something in a storybook. Maybe a fairy tale even.

"It's kind of cold in here," noticed Amy.

"I don't imagine they have any kind of central heating," observed Mrs. Watson. "Old homes like this seldom do."

Just then Cara returned with a disappointed expression. "I am so sorry," she told them. "Miss McPhearson does not know a Mrs. Watson."

Mrs. Watson tapped the side of her head with her forefinger. "Of course not. Goodness, what was I thinking? Please, dear, tell Viola that Martha O'Hara is here to see her. Tell her that I am Margaret O'Hara's younger sister." She peered at Cara. "Can you remember that, dear?"

"Martha O'Hara," Cara repeated. "Margaret O'Hara's sister."

"That's right," said Mrs. Watson. "See if she remembers those names."

They waited again, and Amy was getting even more nervous now. On one hand, she did want to see this strange Viola McPhearson, but on the other hand, what if she got all tongue-tied and nervous and couldn't even remember why it was she'd come here today? Amy hated looking stupid. Then Amy reminded herself of how she'd stood up and done perfectly well in spelling bees, and how she'd performed without a single slipup for the mental-math competition. Why should this be any different? She took a deep breath and steadied herself as Cara returned for the second time.

"Miss McPhearson will see you in the library," she told them, pointing off to her right as she led the way. They followed her down a hallway until she paused by a pair of tall carved doors. Then, pushing one of them open, she nodded into the dimly lit room. Mrs. Watson and Amy went in, but no one was there.

"Please, sit down," Cara told them. "Miss McPhearson will come." Then she left them on their own again.

"I guess we should sit and wait," said Amy. She glanced at Mrs. Watson. "I hope you don't mind. I mean, I didn't know this would take so long and—"

"Don't worry, dear," said Mrs. Watson as she sat in an overstuffed chair next to the unlit, dark fireplace. "I haven't had this much fun in ages."

Amy blinked in surprise as she sat in a straight-backed chair across from her. Did Mrs. Watson really think this was fun? As her eyes adjusted to the dim light, she noticed that the floor-to-ceiling bookshelves were filled with books. Hundreds and hundreds of books. Other than the school and public libraries, she had never seen so many books in one place. "Isn't it lovely," she said suddenly.

"What?" Mrs. Watson looked surprised.

"All these books."

"Oh, yes." She nodded. "Books are rather nice."

"Someday I'll have a house with a library in it," proclaimed Amy. "Oh, maybe not as big as this, but I will have one."

"Good for you."

Just then they heard a noise and looked up to see a shadowy silhouette coming toward them right out of the wall! Amy jumped in her chair, thinking that she was seeing an actual ghost. But the figure made a harrumph sound as it came closer, and Amy realized that it looked more like an old woman. It must be Viola McPhearson.

Amy stood and nearly bowed, but stopped herself. "I'm Amy Ngo," she said quickly. "And this is my friend—"

"Martha O'Hara," Mrs. Watson finished for her as she stood and extended her hand to the elderly woman. "I'm Margaret's younger sister. Do you remember me, Viola?"

Viola ignored Mrs. Watson's hand as she slowly sat in the overstuffed chair on the opposite side of the fireplace. She took her time to carefully arrange her feet on a small footstool. But her expression was grim as she studied the two of them. She had on a gray skirt that matched her hair and a pale blue cardigan sweater that was buttoned all the way up to her sagging double chin. Her nose was long—a bit like a beak—and a pair of thick, oversized glasses seemed to teeter on its bridge, making her eyes appear large and owlish. In a way, she looked kind of interesting, except for her sour expression. It was a little intimidating.

"You're the girl who wrote me the letter," said Miss McPhearson in a voice that sounded almost like a man's. Maybe she was a smoker. Amy remembered an old guy named Hank who came to their restaurant every Thursday night at 6:15. He reeked of tobacco and had a deep, raspy voice that Ly said came from smoking too much.

"Yes," said Amy. "I wrote the note."

"Harrumph."

Amy wondered what the proper response to "harrumph" might be.

"It's been years," said Mrs. Watson in a cheerful voice. "How have you been all this time, Viola?"

Miss McPhearson turned her attention from Amy back to her other guest. She peered at her for a long moment, as if taking her in. "My, but you've certainly gotten old," she said.

Mrs. Watson laughed. "Happens to the best of us, dear."

"Harrumph."

"Did you have a chance to read my letter, Miss McPhearson?" asked Amy hopefully.

"I'm old, not stupid," she snapped back. "Of course I read it."

"Oh."

"So you're aware of the situation with McPhearson Park then," said Mrs. Watson.

"Of course I'm aware."

"You understand that it's been vandalized?"

Miss McPhearson rolled her big owl eyes.

"Do you plan to do something about it?" asked Mrs. Watson.

"I don't see why I should."

"Did you get a letter from the city yet?" asked Amy.

"Don't see how that's any of *your* business." Miss McPhearson leaned forward in her chair and scowled at Amy.

Amy looked over at Mrs. Watson now, thankful that she wasn't facing this Dragon Lady alone.

"Amy and her friends are very concerned about losing the city park," explained Mrs. Watson. "It has always been such a wonderful place for the entire town. It would be a shame to see it go."

"Looks to me as if it's already gone," said Miss McPhearson. "If people want to tear it down and destroy it, why not let them. I certainly don't plan to stand in their way."

"But it is your family's park," tried Amy. "Doesn't that mean anything to you?"

"Don't know why it should."

"But it was always such a beautiful park, Viola. I remember you down at the concerts and dances. You enjoyed it just as much as any of us. Why wouldn't you want to preserve that?"

"Because it's too late. And because I don't care!"

"You really don't care?" began Amy cautiously. "It doesn't bother you that the city wants to turn your family park into a parking lot?"

Miss McPhearson didn't say anything now.

"Maybe they'll call it McPhearson Parking Lot," continued Amy. "And it'll be nothing but boring gray cement, and it'll be dusty and hot —"

"That's enough!" said Miss McPhearson.

"But if you really don't care … " Amy pressed on. "Why should it bother you?"

Miss McPhearson narrowed her eyes as she pointed a gnarled finger at Amy. "You don't know what you're talking about, young lady!"

Amy sat back in her chair. Maybe she had pushed the Dragon Lady too far.

"Now, Viola," said Mrs. Watson in a soothing voice. "It seems that you do care about your family's park, don't you, dear?"

"Harrumph."

"And maybe it does worry you, just a bit, that it could be turned into a parking lot. Just as, I'm sure, it would worry your ancestors as well."

Miss McPhearson shrugged ever so slightly.

"So I don't understand why you wouldn't want to do something to see that the park is preserved — restored — so that future generations might be able to use it and enjoy it."

"Fine. I don't care if the park is preserved. But I don't plan on lifting a finger to help. And I won't spend one single penny on it either. Putting money into that park would be like pouring water down a rat hole."

Amy wasn't sure what that was supposed to mean, but she decided to just ignore it. "My friends and I are willing to work on the park," she said eagerly. "We fixed up our trailer park — we planted green things and cleaned it up — and we can work to fix up the city park too."

"I seriously doubt that."

"We can," Amy insisted. "If you will just give us your permission, I think we can have a lot done within thirty days. You'll see."

She rolled her eyes again. "Do as you please. I won't stop you. But don't come crying to me if it doesn't work out right."

"We won't," promised Amy.

"Good."

"So it's agreed," said Mrs. Watson. "You give the girls your blessing to do what they can to save McPhearson Park."

Miss McPhearson laughed. But there was no happiness in her laugh. More than ever she looked like a real Dragon Lady just now. "My blessing?" she snarled at Amy. "Wouldn't that be a joke!" Then she stood and walked over to where she had emerged from earlier, and Amy could see now that it was some kind of a hidden door where the bookshelf turned and provided a nifty escape. "Good day!" she snapped just before she disappeared.

"Wow," said Amy, letting out a deep breath.

"Wow is right," said Mrs. Watson as she stood up. "You are a brave girl, Amy."

"Oh, I don't know ... " Amy remembered how she'd chickened out of soccer tryouts earlier today. She wondered how her friends had fared. She also wondered what they'd think of her news. She couldn't wait to tell them!

"I hope that it all works out for you and your friends," said Mrs. Watson as they found their way back down the hallway and to the foyer. Cara didn't seem to be anywhere around. Amy hoped that she hadn't gotten in trouble for letting them in. "And I want to make good on my promise to help," she continued. "If you decide to proceed with the Save the Park project, be sure to write me and I'll send you a check. Oh, it won't be much because I'm not rich, but I'll do what I can."

"Thanks," said Amy as they went outside. But instead of going to the car, Amy walked a bit past the front of the house and peeked around the side. "Oh, my!" she said when she saw the gorgeous view of the ocean. "Look at this."

Mrs. Watson joined her. "Yes, the panorama is spectacular here. You should see their backyard, Amy. That is, if it's been kept up all these years."

"I would so love to have a house with a view like this." Amy sighed as she turned and followed Mrs. Watson back to the car.

"I remember seeing a sunset here once," said Mrs. Watson. "So beautiful …"

"I wonder if Miss McPhearson ever enjoys it?" asked Amy as she buckled her seat belt.

"It's hard to say …" Mrs. Watson backed her car out then stopped. "I have an idea, Amy."

"What?"

"It just occurred to me that I still know a few people in this town, people who've been here for nearly as long as Viola. Perhaps I could write some letters to some of them, try to garner a little support for your project."

"That would be great," said Amy.

"Because the more I think about it, the more I think that park needs to be saved. And I want to do whatever I can to help."

Amy felt some of her original enthusiasm returning now. "I can't wait to talk to my friends and tell them that Miss McPhearson said it's okay. When I have a better idea of what we're going to do, I'll get back to you. Okay?"

"That sounds fine."

Amy felt slightly hopeful as they drove back into town. In some ways it seemed it would take a real miracle to accomplish this task. Amy remembered the time, not so long ago, when Carlie and Chelsea had been swept out to sea. Morgan and Emily had prayed for them — asking God for a miracle — while Amy used her cell phone to call for help. And when the girls were rescued, both Chelsea and Carlie believed that it really had been a miracle. Maybe they could pray for another one.

chapter five

"You should've seen the place," said Amy, as she finished telling her friends at the Rainbow Bus the story of her strange visit to Viola McPhearson's house.

"That is so weird," said Carlie. "Weren't you scared?"

"A little," admitted Amy. "But it was pretty interesting too. That house is totally amazing, like something out of a fairy tale … or maybe even a horror movie if it was a dark and stormy night." She laughed.

"You are so lucky," said Chelsea. "I would love to see the McPhearson mansion. I've heard my dad talk about it before. He said it should be in the historical listings and that it's worth millions."

Amy nodded. "It probably is. And it's full of antiques too. It's like a museum. But Miss Viola McPhearson … well, *she* is something else."

"Was she crazy like they say?" asked Emily.

Amy considered this. "No, I don't think she's crazy. But she is really mean and cranky. Cara, the girl who works there, calls her the Dragon Lady. Not to her face, of course. But the name seems to be fitting. Miss McPhearson's tongue is pretty sharp, and she's a little bit scary too."

"But she really said it was okay to fix up the park?" asked Morgan.

"She sort of snarled it out," confessed Amy. "But she basically said we could do as we pleased with the park. She didn't seem to care one way or another … although she doesn't want it to be a parking lot."

"Is that all we need?" asked Carlie. "Just the Dragon Lady's permission?"

"I'm not sure," said Amy. "But at least I had Mrs. Watson there to witness the whole thing. And I have her address and phone number."

"I wonder if we need something in writing," said Morgan.

"I don't see why," said Emily. "If the Dragon Lady says it's okay to fix it up, isn't it okay?"

"I don't know … " Chelsea frowned. "My dad would probably say it wasn't okay. But then he doesn't want the park there anyway."

"I know," said Amy. "And that worries me a little. I think I'll call the mayor again. I'll tell him about my visit with Miss McPhearson and what she said, and I'll tell him that we plan to start cleaning it up on Saturday."

"Hey, let's call Gary Hardwick at the newspaper," said Emily suddenly. "Remember, he did the story about how we fixed up the trailer park. Maybe we can get him to do a story about the Save the Park plan too."

"Great idea," said Amy. "Since you're the writer, why don't you call him?"

"And I'll send my letter to the paper tomorrow," said Morgan. "Maybe it will run on Saturday too."

"Me too," said Chelsea.

"I'll talk to my dad about getting some more permits to dig plants in the woods," said Carlie. "Maybe we can try to do that in the next couple of weeks."

"Yeah," said Morgan. "That'll give us time to earn some money and clean things up a little in the park."

"How exactly do we plan to earn money?" asked Emily.

"Maybe we can sell things," said Carlie.

"Like what?" asked Chelsea.

"Maybe Morgan could help us make some beaded things," suggested Emily. "Everyone is always saying how much they like Morgan's bead necklaces and bracelets."

"And how about cookies," said Amy. "I can get the recipe for my mom's almond cookies. We could probably make them at the restaurant if we did it when it wasn't too busy."

"Hey, what about a car wash?" said Morgan with enthusiasm. "We did that once for our youth group at church. And we earned about a thousand dollars in one day."

"In one day?" said Chelsea. "That's amazing."

"That's it!" said Amy. "We'll pick a Saturday as our big fund-raising day. We can have a car wash and we'll sell beadwork and baked goods and whatever …" She studied the brightly colored calendar that Morgan had brought back from the gift show last summer. "How about September 30? That gives us a week and a half to get it all together. Do you think we can do that?"

Everyone thought that sounded doable. And so it was settled. Emily wrote down all their ideas in the notebook, and everyone was assigned a specific task that they would report back on by Friday. Amy would call the mayor and supervise the bake sale preparations. Morgan would talk to her youth pastor to see about setting up a car wash in town. Emily would contact Gary at the newspaper. And Carlie would arrange for her dad to help them get plants.

"What about me?" asked Chelsea as they were finishing. "I don't have a job to do."

They all looked at her, but no one seemed to have an answer.

"*Flyers!*" said Amy suddenly. "We'll need to advertise what we're doing in the community. And you have that great computer and printer, Chelsea. Can you be in charge of publicity?"

Chelsea grinned. "No problem."

"Okay, you'll have to coordinate with the rest of us, you know, for where and what time the car wash will be and that sort of thing."

"And how about donation boxes?" said Chelsea. "You know, the kind that you put in stores and shops asking people to chip in their spare change to help out?"

"Great idea!" said Amy.

"Yeah," Carlie said with a chuckle. "You could put a box in your dad's bank. There's lots of money in there."

Chelsea laughed. "It's not really my dad's bank, you know."

"This looks like it's really coming together," said Morgan. "We make a good team."

"Speaking of teams, I guess it was a good thing Amy didn't try out for soccer today," said Carlie. "Otherwise, she never would've met the Dragon Lady, and none of this would even be happening."

Amy nodded. "But how did it go at the tryouts this afternoon? Did you guys all make the team?"

Emily laughed. "Yeah, *everyone* who tried out made the team. No one was cut. You would've made it too, Amy."

Amy shrugged. "Well, the truth is I'm not really that into soccer. But I'll come and watch you guys at your games." She laughed. "I'll be your cheerleader."

"You'll also have more time to work on this project now," said Morgan. "In fact, I nominate Amy to be chairperson of the Save Our Park campaign."

"Save Our Park," echoed Emily. "That has a nice ring to it."

"Because it is *our* park," said Amy. "Oh, sure, the Dragon Lady might actually own it, but she doesn't really care about it. We're the ones who care about it. I think that makes it as much ours as hers."

"Well, hopefully we will be able to save it," said Chelsea.

They all voted in favor of Amy being the chairperson for their project, and then the meeting broke up. Feeling happy at her new appointment, Amy went straight home and called the mayor. She caught him just as he was about to leave his office, and he sounded like he was in a hurry. She quickly told him about meeting with Miss McPhearson and how she'd given permission to work on the park.

"She actually *spoke* to you?" His voice sounded skeptical.

"She did. And I even had a witness with me," said Amy in her most adult-sounding voice. "Mrs. Watson. She's an old friend of Miss McPhearson. Her name used to me Martha O'Hara, and she grew up in Boscoe Bay."

"Martha O'Hara?" he repeated. "I believe she married Harry Watson. Yes, I do remember her."

"So our plan is to begin working on the park this weekend," Amy informed him. "We just wanted you to know."

He chuckled. "Well, it's a pretty big job for kids."

"Maybe," she admitted. "But we're hard workers. And we'll be having some fund-raising events too. Look for us in the newspaper on Saturday."

"Yes, I noticed a couple of letters in there today. I guess you kids might be a force to be reckoned with after all."

Amy considered this. "Does that mean we're not on the same side?"

He cleared his throat. "I'm the mayor, you know. I represent everyone in the city."

"I just hope you're representing us too," she said. "We might be kids, but we're part of the city too."

He laughed. "Of course you are."

But as Amy hung up the phone, she wasn't entirely convinced. And when her parents came home later that night, she knew there was reason to be worried. They made it very clear that they were opposed to her involvement in saving the city park. They also told her the restaurant needed that space for parking and she should stay out of it.

"I can't stay out of it," she told them. "I am the chairperson of the Save Our Park project."

They looked at her with surprised disbelief.

"You are so full of yourself," said her mother in Vietnamese. "Such a spoiled child, so self-serving and important. I think you are delusional."

"Are you really a chairperson?" asked her father in a slightly softer tone.

"It's true," said Amy defensively, still speaking in English. "I was elected as the chairperson just today. And I've already spoken to the owner of the park as well as the mayor, and there will be something in the newspaper about our group on Saturday. We plan to do all we can to preserve McPhearson Park."

Her father actually chuckled now. "I did not know we raised a little revolutionary."

But her mother frowned and said, "A disrespectful daughter brings a curse upon her mother."

Amy considered this. Part of her wanted to argue with her mother, but part of her felt hurt too. "Why is trying to save a park so that children can play considered disrespectful?" asked Amy, also in Vietnamese, just in case her mother wanted to pretend not to understand her English. She often did that to her children when she didn't want to participate in their conversation.

Her mother just looked at her, disapproval written all over her face. Naturally, Amy wasn't too surprised when her mother didn't answer. Instead she just turned and went into the kitchen. Amy watched her slightly hunched back as she walked. She looked more tired than usual, and Amy knew that she worked hard at the restaurant every day, probably harder than she needed to. But then her mother had difficulty leaving things to others. She seemed to think the world would fall apart if everything wasn't done her way.

Amy held up her hands and sighed. The truth was she didn't want to be disrespectful to her mother, and she really didn't want to bring a curse onto her. But why couldn't her mother see that Amy and her friends were only trying to make their town into a better place? A better place for everyone. Why did this have to be so hard?

Her father patted her on the head. "Don't worry, little Amy. You know your mother is a stubborn one." Then he winked at her. "And … you, my child, are your mother's daughter."

Amy frowned at him. *Now what was that supposed to mean?* As she went to her room to do homework, she realized she would need to get back on her mom's good side if she wanted to use their kitchen to make cookies for the fund-raiser. At least she had a few days to figure that one out. For now she wanted to do her homework, and to do it as perfectly as possible. It was important for Amy to keep her grades up. Her goal was to graduate from high school with a perfect straight-A average from kindergarten on up. Okay, maybe some people thought that was obsessive, but it was just her way. She liked things to go perfectly.

But as she worked on her algebra she was distracted by thoughts about Viola McPhearson, or rather the Dragon Lady. She wondered why someone who had been born into such a wealthy and influential family, someone who seemed to have everything money could buy — a home worth millions, a beautiful view of the ocean — was so deeply unhappy?

She set down her pencil and wondered if Miss McPhearson might have some deep, dark secret hidden somewhere in that big, old spooky house. Had she murdered someone? Were there dead bodies buried in her basement? Maybe she really was crazy. Or perhaps her parents had been cruel and overbearing to her. Not unlike the way Amy's mother could be at times. Or maybe they beat her and locked in her room. That would certainly make a person mean and angry. But then she remembered what Mrs. Watson had said about the lovely parties that had been held there. That didn't seem to add up. Maybe Viola McPhearson had simply been spoiled.

Amy replayed her own mother's words from today. And how many other times had she been told that she was spoiled and selfish and self-centered? Of course, Amy always flatly denied it. But maybe she was just a little spoiled — at least in some ways. After all, she was the youngest and consequently hadn't been forced to work in the restaurant as much as her older siblings had. But Amy did her part. Didn't she? Sure, maybe she complained at times, but didn't they all?

Even so, Amy thought as a chilly shiver ran down her back, she didn't want to be a spoiled brat. And she sure didn't want to grow up to be as unhappy and mean as the Dragon Lady!

chapter six

The girls met in the clubhouse on Friday after school. Everyone reported on how their assignments were coming, and things seemed to be falling into place.

"Gary Hardwick from the newspaper called me last night," said Amy. "He told me that Emily had phoned and filled him in on most of the details. But he asked me a few questions on the history of the park and my conversation with Miss McPhearson."

"You mean the Dragon Lady," interjected Chelsea.

Amy giggled. "I couldn't very well call her the Dragon Lady to the newspaperman. That wouldn't have sounded very professional. Anyway, he said that he hadn't been able to reach her for an interview."

"He was probably jealous," said Emily.

"I've got the flyers planned out," said Chelsea. "I brought a sample to show you what I have so far. I'll add the time and place when we know them for sure."

"The car wash will be at McDonald's," said Morgan. "Our youth pastor knows the guy who owns the franchise, and he said it'll be okay."

"Cool," said Chelsea as she wrote this down. "That's a great location."

"I thought we could sell the baked goods and things by the park," said Amy. "That way people will see what bad shape it's in ... and maybe they will want to help out."

"Good idea," said Carlie.

"We could put signs at the car wash to tell people to go up there," said Chelsea.

"And signs at the park," said Emily, "to tell people to go to the car wash."

"Yeah!" said Morgan, giving high fives all around. "Are we good at this or what?"

"Gary from the paper said to make sure we get the information about our fund-raising events dropped off by Monday morning if we want to get them into the What's Happening column in Tuesday's paper," said Emily.

"Can you cover that?" asked Amy.

"Got it."

And on they went, asking questions and reporting progress just like one of the Fortune 500 corporations that her father often read about in his business magazines. Amy thought maybe someday she could head a big company like that herself. It could be fun. Wouldn't her parents be proud of her then? Maybe her mother would take back all that nonsense about being spoiled.

"Be prepared to get your hands dirty tomorrow," Carlie said as they were locking up the clubhouse. "My dad offered to give us a lift down to the park. That way we can take all the tools and the wheelbarrow and stuff."

"What we really need is a big old tractor," said Chelsea.

"No . . . " said Amy as she considered this. "Think about it. If the five of us girls are out there working and digging and trying to put things back into place, how will other people feel when they walk by and see us?"

"Guilty?" offered Emily.

"Exactly!" Amy grinned.

"So maybe they'll want to help too?" suggested Carlie.

"Or donate money?" said Chelsea.

"Or just be supportive of the park in general," finished Amy.

"Good plan," said Morgan. "I hope it works."

They met at Carlie's house the next morning at eight. As much as Amy didn't enjoy doing yard work or getting her fingernails dirty, she was ready for this challenge. She had on her old blue jeans, a sweatshirt, her dad's Raiders hat, and even a pair of her mom's gardening gloves.

The other girls looked like they were ready for work too. "Let's go," said Carlie's dad with a wide grin. "You girls have got work to do."

"Did you guys see the newspaper this morning?" asked Morgan as the pickup took off.

"Was Gary's article in it?" asked Carlie.

"More than just that," said Morgan.

"Our letters?" asked Amy.

"More than that … "

"What?" asked Amy, growing impatient.

"There were letters from some of the downtown businesses who are against saving the park." Morgan paused.

"A lot of letters?" asked Amy.

"Six."

"Whoa."

"And there was this big article written by Rich Howard from Howard Hardware saying how much this town needs a parking lot."

"Oh …" Amy frowned. "But what about our article, the one Gary Hardwick wrote?"

"It was there, but on page five."

"Where was the other article?"

"The front page."

"Oh …"

"My mom said it's because Rich Howard is best buddies with Leon Simpson, the owner of *Boscoe Bay News*," continued Morgan. "She said it was probably a boys' club kinda thing."

Mr. Garcia chuckled from behind the steering wheel. "You ladies may have a little battle on your hands."

"The boys' club against the girls' club?" said Amy.

The girls laughed.

Mr. Garcia pulled up to the park, which still had yellow tape around it. "Well, I'll put my money on the girls' club any day."

"Thanks, Dad," said Carlie.

He helped them unload their tools. "I wish I could stick around and help," he told them. "But we're taking the boat out this afternoon ... plan to fish all night."

"That's okay, Dad," said Carlie. "We have a little plan." She winked at Amy.

"What about the tape?" asked Morgan as they stood on the outside looking in.

"Well, I told the mayor we had Miss McPhearson's permission, and he seemed okay," said Amy.

"Hey, you guys!" called Chelsea as her mom pulled up next to them. "Ready to roll?"

"We were just talking about the yellow tape," said Carlie.

"I say it's coming down," said Chelsea as she reached over and gave it a tug. Soon they were all pulling on it, taking it down. Then they made a tool area and gathered to make a plan for how they would attack all this.

"It looks like the city must've done a little work," observed Amy. She pointed over to the swings and lampposts that had been partially pulled down by the vandals. Now they were fully dismantled and lying flat on the ground.

"Probably getting ready to put in the parking lot," said Carlie.

"Not if we can help it," said Amy in a firm voice. "You guys ready to work?"

"I have a suggestion first," said Morgan. "How about if we bow our heads and say a prayer. I have a feeling we're going to need God's blessing to complete this project. Do you guys agree?"

Everyone nodded and said yes. Except Amy. But she bowed her head and pretended she got this. And part of her wanted to get it. It was just that she had never prayed before. More than ever she felt like a foreigner here.

"Dear heavenly Father," prayed Morgan, "we want to take care of this park so that kids and people will have a good place to gather and enjoy the trees and nature and fresh air ... but we need your help to do it. We're only five girls and not all that good at landscaping. Not only that, but it seems there are people who don't want us to succeed. We pray that your hand will be on us now, that you will help us do our work and do a good job. And we pray that when we finish our job, you will be the one to be glorified. We want to do this for you, Lord. We pray this in your name. Amen."

The other girls said "Amen." Even Amy said "Amen." She figured she should be able to do that much. Then they picked up their shovels and rakes and went to work leveling the ground that had been so badly torn up by the vehicles. Their goal was to get it ready for planting grass. Where they would get the grass turf was unsure, but they wanted to get it ready.

"It's too bad that Howard Hardware is against this project," said Morgan as she pushed her glasses back up and wiped the sweat from her brow. "I'd hoped that we could ask them to donate some things."

"Like grass turf," said Carlie.

"Yeah," said Morgan. "But I guess we get to trust God for that. We'll just take it one day at a time."

"How many days do we have left?" asked Chelsea.

"Twenty-three," said Amy. "But that's if you start from the day the vandals hit. If you start from when Miss McPhearson got her letter, it could be more."

"Good that we have the math whiz working for us," said Carlie.

"What's going on there?" called a man's voice from the nearby sidewalk. The girls looked up to see Mr. Howard from the hardware store looking on with a frown on his face.

"We're working," called Amy. "Fixing this place up."

"Who said you could do this?" he asked.

"The owner," Amy shot back as she scooped another shovelful of dirt into the wheelbarrow.

"You expect me to believe you really talked to Viola McPhearson?" he asked as he walked over to where they were working.

Amy stood up straight and looked him squarely in the eyes. "Yes."

"Viola McPhearson had a conversation with you? And she gave you permission to work on this land?"

"That's what I just told you," said Amy.

He scowled. "Well, I just find that difficult to believe."

"Look," said Chelsea, coming over to stand by Amy. "Amy went to Miss McPhearson's house and talked to her. She even has a witness, and it's a fact. We've got work to do here and, unless you plan on helping, why don't you leave us alone."

Amy blinked and stepped back. "Yes," she said in a nervous voice. "That's the truth. If you don't believe me, go talk to Miss McPhearson."

He sort of laughed, but not in a nice way. "That's a good idea, little lady. Maybe I'll do that." Then he walked away, and the girls went back to work. They worked quietly for about half an hour, and suddenly Amy thought of something.

"What if he *does* do that?" said Amy as she drove her shovel in again.

"Who does do what?" asked Morgan.

"What if Mr. Howard goes to see Miss McPhearson?"

"So what if he does?" said Chelsea. "She won't see him, will she?"

"Probably not," said Amy. "But what if she does see him?"

"It's not like she's going to tell him he can have his stupid parking lot, is it?" asked Morgan.

"Probably not," said Amy. "But she is kind of a strange lady."

"Or …" began Emily in a suspicious tone. "What if Mr. Howard tells everyone that he spoke to Miss McPhearson and that she told him she never gave us permission to work here?"

"That could get messy," said Amy as she turned her dad's ball cap around backward. "It would be his word against mine. And he's friends with the newspaper."

"And all the other business owners in town," added Chelsea. "At least the ones who want this park turned into a parking lot."

"You might have to go see the Dragon Lady again, Amy," said Carlie.

Amy swallowed hard. She had no desire to go see the Dragon Lady again. Especially not without Mrs. Watson by her side.

"Well, we don't need to think about that now," said Morgan. "Right now we have work to do. And like Jesus said, we can only live one day at a time. We don't need to worry about tomorrow."

"We just need to keep praying," said Emily.

The others agreed and went back to work. They worked long and hard until noon. Then Chelsea offered to treat everyone to lunch.

"But we're a mess," said Amy.

"No problem," said Chelsea with a grin. "My mom is going to deliver it to us." And at 12:30 Mrs. Landers pulled up with a six-foot-long sub sandwich and drinks and chips for everyone. They cleaned off a beat-up picnic table — one of the few that were still in one piece — and sat down. Morgan said a blessing over the food and they all ate hungrily. Then they went back to work, and by the afternoon it actually looked as if they were accomplishing something. Together they had piled all the broken pieces of equipment over in a corner of the park. They hoped that these things could either be fixed or carried away, but putting them in one area helped to make the rest of the park look less hopeless.

"At least this will be ready for some grass," said Amy as they stepped back and looked at the nicely smoothed field where kids could kick a soccer ball around.

"And maybe we can get some of that free recycled mulch from the dump," suggested Carlie. "I'll ask my dad if—"

"Hey!" called a girl's voice from the sidewalk. "What d'ya retards think you're doing anyway?"

"Yeah, aren't you a little old to be playing in the park?"

Amy stopped raking long enough to observe a couple of girls from their school. And she immediately knew this wasn't good.

"It's Andrea Benson," said Morgan in a hushed tone. "And Jennifer Wagner."

"So?" said Chelsea, who was still new enough in town not to realize that these were two of the meanest girls at Washington Middle School.

"Andrea and Jennifer aren't very nice," Amy whispered to her.

"And that's an understatement," said Emily as she leaned on her shovel and watched. Then a few more girls from school joined Andrea and Jennifer. They had soda cups and stood there looking at the hardworking girls as if they were sideshow freaks.

"Let's get back to work," said Morgan. And the girls turned their backs on their little audience and started shoveling and raking again.

Soon they began taunting them and calling them names.

"Pigs in the park," yelled Jennifer. "You guys are so pathetic."

"Don't you know that no one wants this stupid park?"

"Hey, park pigs," called out Andrea. "Do you guys have any idea how stupid you look right now?"

"Why don't you get down on your hands and knees and use your snouts to dig in the dirt?" called the other girl.

"Why don't you get a life?" yelled Chelsea back.

"Just ignore them," said Morgan loudly enough so the mean girls could hear. "They just wish they had something worthwhile to do too."

"Yeah, right," yelled Jennifer. "Like we'd want to come out there and dig in the dirt like a bunch of retarded park pigs."

Emily held out her hand, pointing to her bracelet to remind her four friends of their secret Rainbow Rule. "Thanks for stopping by," she called out to their spectators in a cheerful voice. "We so appreciate your encouragement."

Then the mean girls just laughed and walked away.

"Way to tell them, Emily," said Morgan.

"Rainbows rule," Emily shot back at her.

Of course, Amy was still fuming. She'd be happy to throw out the Rainbow Rule right now. More than anything, she would've liked to have given those stupid girls a piece of her mind. Who did they think they were anyway? But she suppressed her anger, putting the energy into her raking and shoveling. They'd show them!

Finally the work day was coming to an end and all five girls were exhausted. Amy had three blisters, and despite wearing garden gloves she didn't know if she'd ever get the dirt out from under her fingernails.

"We made some good progress," said Morgan.

"I guess ..." Amy sighed as she looked around the park. "But there's so much to be done."

"It sort of feels like just a drop in the bucket," said Emily.

"I just don't see how we can finish this on our own," said Carlie as she loaded the tools into the wheelbarrow. "I mean, even if we get the grass in and some new shrubs planted there's still the broken playground equipment and the lampposts and picnic tables. That's going to cost a lot."

"And no one really seemed to care much about what we were doing today," added Emily. "Not like we'd hoped they would."

Amy felt worried now. Were her friends getting ready to give up? Sure, she was discouraged too, but they couldn't just give up. "We still have three more weekends to finish this," she said stubbornly.

"And we still have prayer," added Morgan.

Amy studied their leader. She wished she had the nerve to ask Morgan about how that really worked. Like, how did Morgan know how to pray? Who had taught her? Where did she get her faith to believe these things? And how did she know that God really listened to prayers? Amy just didn't get it. Maybe she never would.

But Morgan's grandma pulled up then, honking the horn of her car as she waved to the girls. They lugged their tools and things over to her car. It took three of them to load the wheelbarrow into the back of the station wagon, and they had to leave the window open.

"You girls look like you've had a long day," said Grandma as she drove them back to the trailer park.

"And only twenty-five more to go," said Amy in a discouraged voice.

chapter seven

"I don't know about you guys," said Chelsea at lunchtime, "but I'm getting sick and tired of being called the park pigs by girls like Andrea and Jennifer."

Morgan held up her bracelet. "Just remember rainbows rule and try not to let them get to you." She put a straw in her milk and took a sip.

"That's easier said than done," said Amy as she opened her sack lunch and peered inside. She, for one, was fed up with the taunting and teasing that only seemed to be getting worse. Just then a girl walked by their table and loudly snorted like a pig.

"Wow, that's original," said Chelsea in a sarcastic voice. "We haven't heard that sound before."

It was Wednesday, and everyone at school was fully aware of the park controversy by now. Yesterday's newspaper had another article criticizing the girls' efforts to "save a park that didn't need saving." The article pointed out how Boscoe Bay had suffered economically over the past twenty years and how the only way to grow was to "allow more development." Amy wondered how they considered a parking lot to be development, but according to her own parents it was the only way to grow.

Anyway, it seemed clear that the line had been drawn, and not only the adults were taking sides. Kids had quickly taken sides too. And, unfortunately, it seemed that the kids with the biggest mouths — the so-called popular kids — were solidly on the side of development. It was only the quieter kids — many of them "geeks, freaks, and nerds" — who supported the Save Our Park project.

"I think we're being persecuted for righteousness' sake," said Emily.

"What's that supposed to mean?" asked Amy.

"It means we're getting picked on for doing a good thing," said Morgan. "Our pastor preached about it in church on Sunday."

"But that's so wrong," said Chelsea. "Why should we get picked on for doing a good thing?"

"Because most people think it's the wrong thing," said Amy. "Did you read what Mr. Howard from the hardware store said in the paper yesterday?"

"Yeah," said Morgan in a sad voice. "He thinks you made the whole thing up about Viola McPhearson."

"Isn't that slander?" asked Emily.

"Good question," said Chelsea.

"Well, it's made me realize that I need to write Mrs. Watson and ask her to help us," said Amy. "And ..." She took in a deep breath. "I think I should go to visit Miss McPhearson again."

"The Dragon Lady?" said Chelsea. "You're going to go see her again?"

"It seems like the only way," said Amy.

"When?" asked Morgan.

"Today, after school," said Amy. "I already asked my sister An to drive me up there."

"So she'll go with you, then," asked Emily with concern, "to talk to the Dragon Lady?"

Amy shook her head. "No, she'll just drop me off. She has to work at the restaurant."

"We'd go with you," offered Morgan, "except we have soccer practice, and there's a game tomorrow, so we can't miss it."

"That's okay." Amy forced a brave smile. "I'll be fine."

"But you'll be there all by yourself?" said Carlie, clearly alarmed at this. "Just you and the Dragon Lady?"

"I'll have my cell phone," Amy said quickly. "And Cara should be there working. I can call An if anything goes wrong, and she'll come pick me up."

"What do you think could go wrong?" asked Morgan.

Amy shrugged. "Probably nothing. But I have to admit the place is kind of creepy and spooky, and the Dragon Lady is a little strange. But she may just be eccentric."

"You're so brave," said Emily.

Amy thanked her, but the truth was she didn't feel so brave. Still, she felt this was something that needed to be done. And since she was the one who made contact with the Dragon Lady in the first place, it only seemed right that *she* should contact her again. She just hoped the old woman was in a better mood than last time.

"We'll be praying for you," said Morgan suddenly.

"Thanks," said Amy. "Maybe it will help."

"Maybe?" said Emily. "Of course it will. God can do anything, you know."

Amy nodded. But she didn't really know that. She didn't even know how anyone else could know it.

It seemed that school got over very quickly, and soon Amy was walking into the restaurant, and then she and An were driving up to the McPhearson house.

"Wow, this place looks like a haunted house," said An when she pulled up and parked in front. "You sure you want me to just leave you here?"

Amy swallowed hard. "Well, how about if I go ring the doorbell first, just to make sure that the Dragon Lady's —"

"The Dragon Lady?" exclaimed An. "What kind of place is this?"

"Sorry," said Amy. "I shouldn't call her that. But that's what Cara called her, and it kind of fits."

"Good grief, Amy," said An. "I don't like the sound of this."

Amy forced a laugh. "Really, it's okay. But just let me be sure that Cara's here, okay? And then you can go."

"You're sure?"

Amy tried to appear braver than she felt. "Sure. I'll be fine."

"Okay. You wave to me if you want me to go."

"Right."

"And then call me on your cell when you want to be picked up. I'd stick around, but Mom will have a cow if I don't get back and prep for dinner. Ly won't be back from the dentist until five."

"It's okay, An." Then Amy got out of the car and walked up and rang the doorbell. Like before, she waited several minutes, but then Cara appeared. And although she looked surprised, she didn't seem nearly as shocked as last time. In fact, she almost seemed pleased to see Amy.

"I wondered if I could talk to Miss McPhearson?" Amy asked politely.

Cara nodded. "I think so. Come in."

Amy turned back and waved to An, smiling big so that An wouldn't worry. Then the little red car drove away.

"I'm sorry to disturb her," said Amy as she followed Cara inside. "And I would have called, but I don't have her phone number."

"No one does."

Amy nodded.

"Go and sit in the library," Cara instructed her. "I'll go find Miss McPhearson."

So Amy found her way to the dimly lit library again. But instead of sitting down, she walked over to where some heavy red velvet drapes were hanging and she peeked out between them. To her amazement there was the ocean, big and bright and blue. She wondered why Miss McPhearson didn't open the drapes and enjoy this amazing view. In fact, she was tempted to open them herself, but she had a feeling that could cause problems.

"Snooping, are you?" came a deep voice from behind her.

Amy jumped then turned around. "Sorry," she said quickly. Her eyes hadn't adjusted from the brightness outside to the dark in the room, but she knew by the sound of the raspy voice that it was the Dragon Lady. "You have a beautiful view from this room."

"Harrumph."

"I would think you'd want to open the curtains and enjoy it," continued Amy as she walked over and waited as the Dragon Lady sat down, positioning her feet on the footstool again. Today she had on the same gray skirt, but her cardigan sweater was a plum color.

"Well, go ahead and sit down," snapped the Dragon Lady. "Don't just stand there with your mouth hanging open."

Amy sat down and suppressed the urge to point out that her mouth was NOT hanging open.

"So what is it today?" asked the old woman. "Why are you here, Amy Ngo?"

Amy was a little surprised that she remembered her name. "I wanted to speak to you again," she began, "about the park."

"The park, the park … why all this concern about the silly park?"

"Well, do you read the local newspaper, Miss McP-hearson?"

"Of course not. Why would I bother with such nonsense?"

"Some people in town don't believe that I really spoke to you. They think I made the whole thing up and—"

"That's ridiculous," she snapped. "Of course you spoke to me. What's wrong with those foolish people anyway?" Then she laughed, but in that mean way. "Oh, of course, I know what's wrong with those foolish people—they are complete fools!"

"Mr. Howard from the hardware store questioned whether or not I really spoke with you. He actually sounded as if he was going to come out here himself."

"Rubbish! If Richie Howard ever showed up here, I would have him thrown out on his ear. His father, Richard, was an utter fool, but Richie is far worse. I'm surprised he hasn't run Howard Hardware into the ground by now."

Amy considered this. She'd never been particularly fond of Mr. Howard. Mostly because he had never treated her or her family with any respect. He always acted as if he thought they were going to cheat him. Still, she was surprised that Miss McPhearson didn't like him either.

"Don't worry about him," said Miss McPhearson, waving her hand. "I have no use for fools."

Amy nodded. "I must agree with you on that."

Now Miss McPhearson almost smiled, but it wasn't exactly a pleasant smile. In some ways it was scarier than her grim look. "I suspect that you are not a fool, Amy Ngo."

"I hope not," said Amy. "I'm top of my class and I skipped a grade."

"A very smart girl, eh?"

Amy shrugged as she remembered how many times her mother had chided her about being too proud.

"So how is the work coming?" she asked. "On the park? Have you gotten it all put back together yet?"

Amy gave her a brief report on their progress. "But the community support hasn't been as good as we'd hoped," she said finally.

The Dragon Lady scowled. "Well, I hope you aren't here to beg for money!"

"No, of course not," said Amy. "Not at all. What I'd like is something that would prove we are working on the park with your permission. Something I could take to the newspaper so that they wouldn't keep casting a shadow of doubt over our project."

The Dragon Lady nodded, rubbing her chin as if she were thinking.

"We're having some fund-raisers on Saturday, but if no one trusts us or believes that you have really given us permission … well, I doubt that anyone will help us raise money." She sighed. "And it will take money to replace some of the things that were destroyed."

"Why don't the police make the vandals replace those things?" demanded the Dragon Lady.

"They haven't caught them yet," said Amy. "And, as you know, we only have thirty days to make the park usable."

The Dragon Lady narrowed her eyes now, and Amy imagined sparks coming out of her flared nostrils. "It's all their ploy, isn't it, to get the park out of my hands and into theirs?"

Amy considered this. "It really doesn't seem very fair … I mean, most of the city people haven't been very helpful. And the local businesses certainly aren't supportive."

"Including your own family?"

Amy blinked. It felt as if she were reading her thoughts. Then she nodded. "It's true. My own family, at least my parents and one sister, think the park should become a parking lot."

The Dragon Lady stood up suddenly. She walked across the room to where a large desk was situated in a corner. She sat down at it and pulled out a piece of heavy stationery and began to write. After a few minutes she stood and handed the paper to Amy.

"That should take care of Richie Howard or any of those other ridiculous town folks."

Amy studied the letter. It was hard to decipher the spidery-looking letters at first, but she soon was able to read it.

> To whom it may concern,
>
> I, Viola McPhearson, do hereby give my permission for Miss Amy Ngo and her friends to continue their work to restore McPhearson Park, which is legally my property. Any further questions regarding this should be forwarded to my attorney, Mr. William C. Langley.
>
> Sincerely,
>
> Miss Viola McPhearson

"Thank you very much," said Amy.

"But one thing," said Miss McPhearson, pointing a gnarled forefinger just inches from Amy's nose, "you and your friends better not let me down."

Amy didn't know what to say now. Surely this woman realized that they were only five girls, and that the restoration of the city park was a huge task.

"I mean it," said the old woman. "I'm depending on you now."

Amy blinked. "We'll do the best we can, Miss McPhearson. But it's not easy with all the resistance we've been getting."

"Harrumph!"

"Right," said Amy. "Exactly how I feel too."

Then Miss McPhearson laughed. And for a change it almost sounded like a happy laugh. But when Amy looked at her face, she was scowling more deeply than before.

"I won't take up any more of your time," said Amy nervously.

"Just one minute," insisted Miss McPhearson. "I have something else I want you to agree to ... "

Amy was getting worried now. What was she getting herself into with this crazy old woman? Maybe she should just return the letter and run.

"Or perhaps I'll have to take back my letter." She held out a wrinkled hand.

"What is it?" Amy asked cautiously.

"I want you to bring your friends here to meet me," said the Dragon Lady with a sly look in her eye. "I want to see what kind of people I've aligned myself with on this project."

"I ... uh ... I'm not sure they can come."

The Dragon Lady took in a sharp breath. "Then give me back that letter, Amy Ngo. I can't trust you."

Amy stepped back from her. "Okay," she said. "I'll see if I can get them to come here."

"Good. Sunday for tea. Four o'clock sharp."

"If they can come," said Amy.

"You bring them here!" And then she turned and, using her tricky exit from the library, she disappeared into the bookshelf.

Amy took in a slow, steadying breath as a chill like icy fingers ran down her spine. She wanted out of this place — and now! She phoned An as she went out into the foyer, telling her she was ready to be picked up.

"The sooner the better," she told her sister.

"Everything okay?" asked An in a concerned voice.

"Yes. I just want to go home or to the restaurant or anywhere but here. Okay?"

"I'm on my way."

chapter eight

As An drove Amy home, she questioned her about her visit with the Dragon Lady, but Amy didn't really want to talk about it. In fact, she didn't really want to talk at all. Something else was bugging Amy. Something she didn't know if she'd ever be able to talk about. Questions ... too many questions. Nagging, nagging, nagging ...

"Did she frighten you?" asked An after they'd both been quiet for a while.

"Who?"

"The Dragon Lady."

"Oh, not really. Well ... sort of." Amy looked out the window and let out a deep sigh of frustration.

"Are you okay, Amy? You don't seem like yourself today."

"What does it mean to be a Christian, An?" she asked almost without even meaning to. And as soon as the words were out, she wished she could pull them back in.

"Huh?"

"Oh, nothing ..."

"No, Amy. You asked me a serious question. You just caught me by surprise is all. *What does it mean to be —*"

"Like, how did you decide to do it?" she persisted. "I mean, how did you know what to do? Or how to do it? What's it all about? I just don't get it."

An laughed. "Slow down. Too many questions, little sister."

"Sorry." Amy leaned back into the seat. "It's just that all my friends — even Chelsea, who's not always very nice — are Christians. I'm the only one who isn't. And I don't even know how to pray or anything. I just don't get it."

"Uh-huh."

"And I know you're a Christian, An. Even though you don't talk about it very much. But I know you go to a Christian church and you have some Christian friends. I'm guessing even your doctor friend is a Christian."

"That's right. But the reason I don't talk about it much is because of Mom and Dad."

"Did they tell you not to?"

"Not exactly. But I know it bothers them, Amy. And I don't want to make them feel badly. Still, my faith is real. And I can't change it because of them."

"But how did you find it, An? How did you know what to do? I just don't get it."

An laughed. "That's probably because you're trying to get it with your head, Amy. It's not really a head thing."

"Then what is it?"

"It's a heart thing. It's something deep inside of you, Amy. It's like you get this really hungry feeling deep inside.

This longing for something ... someone ... more than what you have. It's a deep spiritual hunger and thirst."

"Yeah?" Amy felt excited now.

"And it's like you can't rest until you find the thing ... the person ... who can fill that place inside of you."

"Yes! Yes!" said Amy. "I feel like that!"

An was pulling into the restaurant parking lot now. She turned and looked at Amy. "Really? You feel like that?"

"Yes. I feel like something inside of me is missing. Like everyone else is in on this really good secret and I'm on the outside. And I feel sort of sad and scared. I can't really explain it, An. But something is really bugging me."

"It's the way God made us, Amy. He made us with a need to have him in our lives. And it's why he sent his Son, Jesus, into the world, so that we could invite him into our hearts and be forgiven and have a real relationship with God."

"But how do you do it?"

"You mean, how do you invite Jesus into your heart?"

"I guess that's what I mean."

"You just do it, Amy."

"How?"

"You pray. Do you want me to pray with you?"

Amy looked down at her lap. She wasn't even sure what she was getting herself into, but she knew she had to take this next step. "Yes."

"All right," said An in a serious voice. "This is how they do it at my church. I'll pray something and you repeat it, but imagine you're talking to Jesus. Okay?"

"Okay."

So An began to pray and Amy followed. And to her surprise it really wasn't all that complicated. But even more surprising was how much better she felt when they were done.

"That's it?" she said.

An laughed. "Good grief, Amy, you just invited the King of Kings into your heart. Don't act too casual about it."

"That's not what I mean," said Amy. "I'm just surprised it was that simple."

"But did you mean it?" asked An. "Did you really mean those words you prayed, in your heart?"

"Of course." Amy nodded. "I wouldn't have prayed them if I didn't mean it."

"Good." An stuck out her hand and shook Amy's. "Welcome to the family of God. You are a Christian, Amy."

Amy smiled. "Cool."

"Yes, cool." An glanced at her watch. "But I better get in there before Mom wigs out. Are you working tonight?"

"Do you guys need me?"

"No. Ly should be back by now."

"And I have homework." Amy grabbed her backpack. "I'll just walk home."

An grinned at Amy. "That really is cool, Amy. I mean, that you're a Christian now." She hugged her. "Now I have someone else in the family I can talk to about this stuff. Wanna go to church with me on Sunday?"

"Sure."

Then they said good-bye and Amy started toward home. But as she walked, she noticed a definite lightness in her step. It felt as if some heavy load had been lifted from her. She couldn't even totally understand it. At least not with her head. But like An had said, she thought she understood it in her heart. She couldn't wait to tell Morgan and the others!

As she hurried home, she decided to try out the praying thing on her own. And since she was still feeling a little concerned about their park project, she decided to pray about that. First, she asked God to help them finish what they had started. Then she reminded him of how the little kids in town really did need a place like that to play in. And she promised God that she would do her best to see that it got finished too. Then she said, "Amen!"

"Hey, Amy!" called a girl's voice, and Amy turned around to see Morgan, Carlie, and Emily hurrying toward her.

"We thought that was you," said Emily as they jogged up and joined her at the entrance to the mobile-home court.

"How'd it go with the Dragon Lady?" asked Carlie.

"You look like you're still in one piece," said Morgan. "We prayed for you."

"Thanks," said Amy. "It went okay. She even wrote me a letter to prove that we really do have her permission."

"Cool," said Morgan.

"Except for one thing," remembered Amy. "She made me promise her something."

"Did she make you write it in blood?" teased Emily.

Amy laughed. "No, but it involves you guys. And Chelsea too."

"What?" asked Carlie.

"The Dragon Lady wants us all to come to tea at her house on Sunday at four o'clock."

"Cool," said Emily, rubbing her hands together. "I can't wait!"

"Really?" Amy was surprised.

"Yeah, me too," said Morgan. "This will be interesting."

"I'm in," said Carlie. "And I know Chelsea will be too. She really wants to see that house."

"Great!" Amy smiled. She had no idea it would be that easy to get her friends to go to the Dragon Lady's. Hopefully they wouldn't all end up locked in her basement.

"So, did you take the letter to the newspaper yet?" asked Emily. "For verification?"

"And to remind them that there are laws against slander?" added Morgan.

"Yeah, that Mr. Howard practically called you a liar," said Carlie. "That's not right."

Amy slapped her forehead. "I totally forgot."

"Well, it's not five o'clock yet," said Morgan. "They'll still be open."

Amy nodded. "I better head back to town right now."

"I'll walk back with you if you want," offered Morgan.

"Me too," said Emily.

"I would love to go too," said Carlie, "but Mom wants me to watch the boys when I get home."

So Amy, Morgan, and Emily told Carlie good-bye then turned back toward town.

"Thanks, you guys," said Amy as they hurried along. "And this gives me the chance to tell you my big news ..."

"About the Dragon Lady?" asked Emily with dramatic interest.

"Bigger than that."

"Bigger?" Morgan looked interested too.

"You'll never guess what I did today."

"Did you get skipped another grade?" asked Morgan.

"No." Amy shook her head. "Bigger than that."

"Did you win the lottery?"

"Bigger."

"*Bigger?*" said Morgan and Emily in unison. Then they looked at each other and back at Amy with bewildered expressions.

"What?" demanded Morgan. "What did you do?"

"I invited Jesus into my heart."

"No way!" yelled Morgan, a huge smile breaking across her face.

"Way!" said Amy.

"Congratulations!" said Emily, squeezing her hand. "Welcome to the real club!"

Morgan hugged her. "Congratulations, Amy. That means we really are sisters now, you know?"

"We're in the same family," added Emily.

"I know." Amy smiled. "And it's so cool."

She told them about her conversation with An and how she prayed with her and how much better she felt already. And suddenly they were at the newspaper office.

"I'm Amy Ngo," said Amy as they stood in front of the reception desk. "I'm the chairperson of the Save Our Park project, and I'd like to speak to the editor, please."

"The editor?" echoed the older woman with a slightly amused expression.

Amy nodded firmly. "Yes, this has to do with something in yesterday's newspaper. Something that might be considered slanderous."

"Slanderous?" The woman looked really curious now. "Why don't you girls go have a seat, and I'll see if Mr. Simpson is available."

They went over to the chairs in the waiting area and sat down.

"Are you nervous?" asked Emily.

Amy considered this. "No, not really."

Morgan grinned. "That's because you have Jesus in your heart, Amy. He can help you through anything."

"Mr. Simpson will see you, Miss Ngo."

Amy looked at her friends. "Can they come too?"

The receptionist shrugged. "I don't see why not."

"I need witnesses," Amy whispered to her friends as the receptionist led them to an office in the back. Emily giggled.

"Amy Ngo," said Mr. Simpson as he stood and shook her hand. "A pleasure to meet you."

Then Amy introduced her friends and they all sat down.

"Mrs. Flynn said that you mentioned a concern about slander," he continued. "Would you care to elaborate?"

So Amy calmly reminded him of the article in yesterday's paper and how Mr. Howard said that Amy might be making up the story about speaking with Viola McPhearson.

He cleared his throat. "Well, you must admit that it sounds a bit far-fetched. I'm not suggesting that you actually lied. But no one in this town, including the mayor, who has made attempts, has spoken to Miss McPhearson for years. For all we know, the woman could've passed on by now. And it's reasonable to assume that a young girl might not have her story straight."

Amy was beginning to fume now. She felt her face growing warm at what sounded like a fairly direct accusation.

"Amy is *not* a liar," interjected Morgan.

Mr. Simpson held up his hands as if he wasn't convinced.

"*And* she has proof," added Emily.

"That's right," said Amy. She stood up and removed the letter from her backpack and laid it on his desk.

He adjusted his glasses and slowly read the scrawled handwriting. Then he looked at Amy and smiled. "This is very interesting."

Amy reached over and took the letter back. "I'd be happy to let you have a copy of this, but I will be holding on to the original."

He chuckled. "You're quite an impressive young lady."

"So if you could print an article that will set the public straight," continued Amy, "we would be most appreciative."

He actually laughed now. "Please, accept my sincere apologies," he told her. "I will do all I can to retract the impression of that other article." He leaned forward. "Would you like to tell me a little about Miss Viola McPhearson? Why she has ignored the city attorney's letter? Or why she isn't involved in the restoration of her own park? Is she helping out financially?"

"Miss McPhearson is a very private person," said Amy. "That's all I can say about that."

He nodded. "Fine. I can respect that."

"I look forward to reading the newspaper on Saturday," said Amy, standing.

"How about a copy of that letter?" asked Mr. Simpson.

"No problem," said Amy.

"I'll ask Mrs. Flynn to make one," he said.

"Thank you."

He smiled. "Thank *you*."

The copy was made, and the girls left the newspaper office. After walking about a block and a half, all three of them burst into giggles.

"Amy Ngo!" exclaimed Morgan. "You were cooler than a cucumber in there."

"I thought you'd turned, like, thirty years old when you were talking to him," gasped Emily between giggles.

Amy laughed. "I just wanted to be sure he took me seriously."

"I think he did," said Morgan.

"You don't think he was laughing at me?" asked Amy.

"Not at all. I think he was totally impressed," said Emily. "I know I was."

Amy felt like she had wings on her feet as they walked home. She couldn't remember when she'd been so happy.

chapter nine

Amy got up early on Saturday morning. It was the day of their big fund-raising events. She had spent the past two afternoons making cookies for the bake sale, and now they were neatly sealed in plastic bags, stacked in a cardboard box, and ready to be sold. She hurried to dress, then went outside to get the newspaper, dodging between raindrops as she hurried back into the house. She opened the slightly damp paper, hoping to see the article promised to her by the editor, but it wasn't on the front page. And, as she searched through the whole thing, it wasn't on any page. So she went to the editorial section, looking for Carlie's letter, the one Emily helped her to write last week. But it wasn't there either. However, there were a couple of letters in support of the parking lot and "continued development in Boscoe Bay." She closed the newspaper and growled. Mr. Simpson had tricked her!

She was still angry when she met her friends at Morgan's house. The girls hovered together under Morgan's carport, watching as rain poured so hard that it overflowed the gutters and splashed onto the ground all around them.

"Not a very good day for a car wash," said Carlie with a frown.

"Maybe it doesn't matter," said Amy sadly. "Did you guys see today's paper?"

"I did," said Morgan. "No article about Miss McPhearson's letter."

"I know." Amy scowled. "And I didn't see any announcement about our fund-raising events in the What's Happening section."

"Me neither."

"This is totally unfair," said Carlie. "How can we do these things if the newspaper won't even cooperate?"

Morgan pointed to the rain. "Even the weather's not cooperating."

"I thought God was supposed to listen to our prayers," said Amy.

"He listens," said Morgan. "But his answers don't always come just as we'd like them to."

"Sometimes we have to wait," said Emily.

"Like my mom says," offered Carlie, "when God closes a door, sometimes he opens a window."

"Who needs an open window on a day like this?" said Amy.

They laughed.

"So what should we do?" asked Morgan. "My grandma is still willing to drive us to town. My youth pastor will bring the car wash stuff for us."

"Chelsea already put up the flyers," said Carlie. "They looked really good too."

"They're probably soggy by now," said Emily.

"I think we should go for it," said Amy suddenly.

"Okay," said Morgan.

So Morgan's grandma drove them through the rain to town. "You sure you girls will be okay?" she asked as she pulled into the back of McDonald's where some hoses and things were already set up and ready to go.

"We've got our raincoats," said Morgan.

"And umbrellas," said Amy.

"Well, be sure and call if you need a ride home," she told them as they all climbed out of the car.

Because of the weather, they decided to keep their fund-raising efforts together in one place. They would wash whatever cars happened to show up and sell cookies and the few beaded bracelets they'd had time to make. But as they stood behind McDonald's, out there in the drenching rain, Amy felt more and more humiliated. The other girls were in good spirits as they joked and laughed at how ridiculous they must appear.

But as the minutes on the clock slowly ticked by, it seemed that hardly anyone was coming — why would they? The rain kept falling, and Amy felt certain their entire day was just a big waste of time. By noon the girls were soaked to the skin, and even the free cocoa from McDonald's wasn't helping. They had washed two cars and sold a couple of packets of cookies and one beaded bracelet for a grand total of $17.25.

"This is crazy," said Chelsea as she shook the water off her raincoat. "I'm ready to call it a day."

"Me too," admitted Morgan. "Washing cars on a rainy day is nuts."

"And my cookies are starting to get soggy," admitted Amy. "I think we should pack it up."

"Maybe we can try again next week," said Carlie.

"Yeah," said Amy, but she was thinking that if they had to wait until next week to raise money, they would only have one weekend left to do the remaining work on the park. Still, they couldn't very well work on the park without money to purchase the things they needed. She didn't want to admit it, but everything about this project was looking too big and too impossible. As they loaded their stuff back into Morgan's grandma's car, she was on the verge of tears, but being the chairperson of this group, she knew she had to hold it in. And so she silently prayed.

"Let's meet at the clubhouse later," said Morgan cheerfully. "After everyone has had a chance to dry off and get some lunch. How about two o'clock?"

They agreed and took off to their separate homes. No one was at Amy's house, which wasn't unusual. Amy was accustomed to having her parents gone most of the time. The restaurant really was their second home. In fact — as Amy had been told dozens of times — her family used to actually live in the small apartment above the restaurant. Now it was used for storage. But that happened long before she was born. And according to her mother, Amy had been born "after life got easy." Probably another reason her mother thought she was spoiled. But today, Amy wasn't sure she agreed with her mother's definition of "easy."

Amy showered and changed and warmed up some leftover fried rice and chicken, eating it while standing and looking out the window, just staring at the never-ending rain. "Why did it have to rain today, God?" she asked between bites. "Couldn't you have given us sunshine instead?"

Then she finished up and headed over to the bus. Morgan was the only one there so far, and she was already busily beading. But Amy was glad to go inside and flop down on the couch, and before long the other girls joined them. Even Chelsea had begged her mom to drive her back over and drop her off. And for the rest of the day they just hung together, making beaded necklaces and bracelets and eating some of Amy's cookies. They listened to old vinyl records and the sound of the rain steadily beating on the roof of the bus, but no one spoke about the city park or the unfinished project. In some ways the atmosphere reminded Amy of a funeral. Not that she'd been to many. But it felt as if something had died today ... maybe just her dream.

On Sunday afternoon, Chelsea's mom gave them a ride up to Viola McPhearson's house. "I wish I could see it too," she said as she dropped them off in the driveway and looked up at the tall dark house.

"Sorry, Mom," said Chelsea. "But we're the only ones invited."

Her mom laughed. "Well, you girls have fun, and call me when you need a ride home."

The girls slowly walked up to the front door. Amy couldn't help but think this was a total waste of time. Especially since the editor hadn't even used Miss McPhearson's letter in the paper yesterday. Right now, Amy held very little hope that they would be able to finish the park renovation on time. Maybe she should just be up front with Miss McPhearson — simply explain that things weren't going so well and apologize for failing.

"This place is really spooky," said Morgan as Amy rang the doorbell.

"I think it's *mysterious*," said Emily with a sly grin. "I could write a great short story about a place like this."

"I think it's cool," said Carlie as she looked at a gangly rosebush. "But the Dragon Lady needs to hire someone to tend her yard. It's really overgrown."

"Remember not to call her that," Amy warned.

Just then Cara opened the door and ushered them in. But instead of going to the library, Cara took them to a different room. Maybe it was a parlor. Amy wasn't sure. But unlike the dark library, this room was a bit lighter, and the heavy velvet drapes were fully open to reveal what would be a stunning view of the ocean if it wasn't all gray and dreary out there.

"Sit down," said Cara. "Miss McPhearson will come soon."

"This looks like the set of a movie," said Chelsea as she sat in a chair covered with faded tapestry. "All this old stuff."

"Can't you just imagine a stack of dead bodies down in the basement?" whispered Emily. "Old bones with chains shackled around them and —"

"Emily!" Morgan used a warning tone. "I've already got the creeps, thank you very much."

Emily giggled. "Sorry."

Just then Miss McPhearson came into the room. Once again, she had on the same gray skirt, but her cardigan was pale pink today, and she'd taken the time to tie a scarf around her neck.

"Hello, ladies," she said in her low, gruff voice. "I see that you've made yourselves comfortable." She looked at Amy. "Are you going to introduce me to your friends, Amy Ngo?"

Amy stood and formally introduced her friends to Miss McPhearson.

"You are quite a mixed bag, aren't you?" said Miss McPhearson as she sat down in a big red armchair. "Not that I'm a bigot. I'm not. I am a very open-minded woman."

Amy frowned at her.

"Oh, have I offended Amy Ngo?" asked Miss McPhearson. "And here I thought you were a woman who liked to speak her mind too?"

Amy looked directly at Miss McPhearson now. "You're right, I do like to speak my mind. But I know as well as anyone that my words can be offensive if I'm not careful."

"That's true," said Morgan, winking at her. "Amy has offended me a few times."

"Me too," said Emily.

"So perhaps Amy Ngo and I have a similar problem," said Miss McPhearson with a slightly wicked-looking smile.

"You have a lovely home," said Carlie.

"Really?" Miss McPhearson peered at her through her big, thick glasses. "You like it?"

Carlie nodded. "Yes. But I think you should hire a landscaper."

"You could hire Carlie," suggested Emily. "She's an excellent gardener."

"She is?" Miss McPhearson looked from one to the next. "I'm starting to think you are some extraordinary young ladies." Her gaze stopped on Amy. "Just what makes you all so special, I'd like to know?"

Amy considered this. "Maybe it's because we're friends."

"Friends," said Miss McPhearson. "Harrumph."

Emily giggled.

"You think I'm funny?"

"No," said Emily quickly. "I just get the giggles sometimes. Usually when I'm nervous."

"Well, tell me, Emily Adams, what is special about you?"

Emily stared blankly back at her.

"I'll tell you what's special about Emily," said Morgan. "She writes poetry and short stories, she solved a big mystery, and she's an excellent friend."

Miss McPhearson nodded, looking at Morgan now. "So, what is special about you, Morgan Evans? What sets you apart?"

"She's a designer," said Carlie quickly. "She designs jewelry and clothes, and she made our bus look totally cool."

"Your *bus*?" Miss McPhearson frowned. "You girls aren't old enough to drive a bus."

So Amy explained the bus clubhouse. The other girls contributed some information, and then Cara brought the tea things in. It became very quiet as the girls drank tea and ate cookies. And finally Miss McPhearson stood up. "That will be all," she said. "I am worn out and need my rest."

Amy blinked, but remembered her manners and thanked her for inviting them to tea. The other girls thanked her too. And then Miss McPhearson left.

"Guess I better call my mom," said Chelsea.

"I told you," said Amy, "she's kind of different."

"I like her," said Emily. "I think she's interesting. And I think she has some tragic story for why she lives all alone like this. I think perhaps she had a true love who went off to war and never came home."

"Maybe his name was Dan Watterson," teased Morgan.

"Who's that?" asked Chelsea.

"Mr. Greeley's son. The one who died in the Gulf War," said Emily. "And no, it wouldn't be him. He'd have been half her age. Her true love would've died in a different war."

"Like maybe the Civil War," teased Carlie.

The girls all chattered as Chelsea's mom drove them back into town, telling her about all the antiques and how the staircase went up several stories and how strange the Dragon Lady was, but that she also seemed interesting. Everyone talked except for Amy.

Amy just wanted to think. Although she wasn't quite sure what to think — about anything. She had meant to tell Miss McPhearson about their disappointing fund-raising efforts yesterday, to prepare the old woman for the possibility that they might not succeed at their project — to warn her that in a couple of weeks there could be city bulldozers turning the McPhearson Park into an ugly parking lot. Of course, Amy hated to admit failure at anything. In fact, she couldn't even remember the last time she had actually failed. Still, there seemed no way to make this thing work out right. She might as well accept it.

She did wonder how God fit into this picture. How could it be that she had prayed — they all had prayed — and things still didn't seem to be turning out right? But here was the really strange part — she didn't feel totally bummed by this. Oh, sure, she was humiliated and didn't like admitting failure, but it wasn't the end of the world. Maybe it was because God was changing something inside her. Or maybe it was because she'd gone to church with An this morning, and everyone there had been so warm and welcoming to her. But whatever it was, she knew something was different, and it was a good kind of different. And despite this total sense of failure, she knew she was going to be okay.

chapter ten

It rained for a solid week. So much so that standing water made it impossible to do anything in the park on Saturday. Not that the girls could do much since they had no money. And it was too wet to drive up the muddy logging roads into the woods to get plants.

"It looks totally hopeless," said Amy as the girls met on Saturday afternoon. "I think it's time to give up on Save Our Park."

"The park looked like a great big lake when we drove through town just now," said Chelsea. "My mom thinks it might be just as well."

"My parents are happy too," said Amy sadly. "My mother is already counting how many cars can fit into the new parking lot."

"Well, at least the editor ran an apology to Amy today," said Morgan. "Did you guys see the paper?"

"Yeah," said Chelsea, "a little late, don't you think?"

"He said it was a slipup," said Amy.

"Whatever..."

"It was a nice article," said Emily. "It actually sounded as if he was sorry."

"It was still too late," said Chelsea.

"My dad said the weather is supposed to change tomorrow," said Carlie. "It's supposed to be sunny all week."

"Great," said Amy. "The park will probably be nice and dry just in time for the bulldozers to move in and flatten the whole thing."

"My dad said he could take us to the woods on Monday," continued Carlie, the only one who still seemed to be holding on to hope. "It's Columbus Day, you know, no school. We could dig up some things to transplant into the park."

"What good would that do?" asked Chelsea.

"I don't know … " Carlie frowned. "But it might be fun."

"Our last-ditch effort," said Morgan with a sigh.

"Let's do it!" said Amy suddenly. "Sure, it might be a waste of time, but let's do it. One last effort."

"We'll go down fighting," said Chelsea, catching her enthusiasm.

"That's the spirit," said Carlie. "And I was looking at that spot where the park sign used to be and thought we could put it back into place and plant some things around it. And I have some flowers I can transplant from my own garden. I mean, I know it's a small thing, but maybe people would see it and get the idea that it could be a pretty place again."

"It's worth a try," agreed Morgan.

"If nothing else, it could be like a memorial to the park," said Emily in a solemn tone. "A reminder to everyone of what could've been."

So it was decided they would meet at Carlie's house at seven on Monday morning. Amy had little hope that it would make any difference, but she did like Chelsea's comment about going down fighting. Why not?

The girls worked harder than ever on Monday morning, each of them fully filling their permit limit with plants they dug from the woods. They brought bag lunches and ate on the road as Mr. Garcia drove them back to town. By the time they were at the park, the sun was shining warmly overhead, and even though the ground was still pretty soggy, it did make the digging easier. Carlie's dad stayed to help, and by six o'clock they had all the shrubs and trees replanted.

"It looks really pretty," said Amy as they stood back to look at the entrance to the park.

"I can't believe it," said Chelsea. "It looks like a professional landscaper was here."

"Carlie's flowers really brighten it up too," said Morgan.

Then Amy looked out at the rest of the park, which still looked a bit like a war zone. "If only we had enough time to get to the rest of it."

"There's no way," said Chelsea. "I mean, this little corner here took us a whole day to do. We don't have money and we don't have time … There's no way."

"It is kind of like a memorial," said Emily.

"Let's pray," said Morgan.

Then all five girls joined hands, and Morgan led them in a prayer. "Dear heavenly Father," she said, "we've done everything we could to preserve this park, but it's just not enough. We know that you're able to do anything, and we believe that if you want to save this park, you can make it happen. You are God of the impossible, and as far as we can see, this project really is impossible. So we give it to you now. Amen."

The other girls said "Amen," and Carlie's dad backed up his pickup so they could start loading their tools into it. But before they got in, they heard someone calling them. "Wait up!"

They turned to see Gary Hardwick from the newspaper approaching them. "Hey, Amy! Can I get a photo of you guys?"

Amy looked at her friends. They were all covered with mud, literally from head to toe. "We're not really looking our best," she told him.

He grinned. "It's okay. You've been working hard. And I thought maybe I could run another little story in the paper about what you've tried to do."

"Even though we failed?" asked Amy.

He frowned. "Well, maybe it'll make some of these businesspeople think."

"Okay," said Amy.

"It'll give the kids at school something to talk about," said Chelsea. "They already call us the park pigs, and today we really look like it."

"They call you the park pigs?" asked Gary as he adjusted his camera lens.

"Yeah," said Morgan. "Most of the mouthiest kids at school think this town needs a parking lot too."

"It's been an uphill battle all the way," said Amy.

"That's too bad," he said. "Okay, now squeeze together a little closer and say cheese." They complied and he took the shot. "I'll try to get this story into Tuesday's paper," he told them.

"But don't hold your breath," said Chelsea after he walked away.

"Right," said Emily. "We know how that goes."

"There's my mom," said Chelsea. "See ya later!"

They all piled back into Mr. Garcia's pickup. Everyone was very quiet as he drove them home. Amy wasn't sure if it was because they were tired or because they were discouraged. She wasn't even sure that she cared.

On Sunday afternoon Amy asked An to drive her back up to the McPhearson house. "I need to tell Miss McPhearson that we've let her down," she told An as they drove.

"It wasn't your fault," said An. "You guys did everything you could."

"I know … but I assured her that we could do this. And now it seems like we've failed."

"Do you want me to wait for you this time?" asked An as she pulled into the driveway.

"Yes," said Amy. "This shouldn't take long."

Cara showed Amy to the library, and before long Miss McPhearson came in. "Hello, Amy Ngo," she said in a voice that almost sounded cheerful. At least for her.

"Hello, Miss McPhearson," said Amy. "I've come with bad news."

She frowned. "What is it?"

"We can't save the park."

"Oh." She waved her hand. "I knew that."

"You knew that?"

"How could five little girls possibly do all that work?"

Amy shrugged. "It seemed possible at the time."

"Well, *now* you know."

Amy studied her. "What do I *know*?"

"That it doesn't pay to dream big, little girl."

Amy blinked. "I'm sorry, but I don't *know* that."

"Well, the sooner you learn *that* lesson, the better off you will be."

Amy stood up and planted her hands on her hips. "I don't think I ever want to learn that lesson, Miss McPhearson. I mean, I know that not all my dreams can come true. But some of them can."

"Harrumph."

"My family came to this country with a big dream." Amy couldn't believe she'd just said this. She'd heard this story enough times from her parents, but it wasn't something she usually talked about. "My parents escaped Vietnam during the war. They weren't much older than me when they fled their homeland with only the clothes on their backs. They had both come from good families, families who had money and wealth but lost everything in the war. My parents lived as refugees for years, practically starving to death. But they eventually got jobs and they got married and even had some kids. But they still had a dream that was bigger than that. They wanted to come to America. They wanted to start a business and put their kids through college." Amy could feel tears in her eyes as she said this. "It was *their* dream, and a lot of their friends thought it was impossible. But they did it, Miss McPhearson. And because of that, I refuse to believe that dreams can't come true."

Miss McPhearson looked slightly stunned, but she didn't say anything.

"And there's an even bigger reason I believe dreams can come true now," continued Amy. "I just invited Jesus into my heart, and I believe that he can do anything and that he can make dreams come true — even if they are impossible."

"Well . . ."

"And I'm sorry if my park dream can't come true, Miss McPhearson. But I will NEVER stop dreaming. Thank you very much!"

And then Amy walked out. Okay, she knew it was rude, but it seemed better than standing there yelling at the woman. Because Amy was mad. What right did Miss McPhearson have to tell Amy that dreams never came true!

"Are you okay?" asked An as Amy stomped out to the car.

"Just fine," snapped Amy. Then she laughed. "Actually, I am. I'm just fine, An."

"Well, good," said An as she drove away. "I thought maybe the Dragon Lady got to you."

"She sort of did," admitted Amy. "But in a good way."

chapter eleven

"It's a miracle," Amy told her friends as they met for an emergency meeting on Friday afternoon.

"What?" demanded Morgan. "Tell us!"

"We have money to finish the park."

"Money?" questioned Chelsea. "What kind of money?"

"Lots of money," said Amy.

"Explain," said Emily.

"Okay, for starters I got this letter from Mrs. Watson today," said Amy, holding up the letter. "She didn't get my address right so it was lost in the mail for a couple of weeks, but it came today. And there was a check in it."

"For how much?" asked Carlie.

"It's for two hundred dollars," said Amy.

"Wow," said Emily.

"Two hundred dollars is not enough to finish the park," pointed out Chelsea.

"I know," said Amy. "But that's not all. Mrs. Watson wrote in her letter that she and some of her friends in town have set up a Save Our Park fund. In your dad's bank, Chelsea!"

"It's not *his* bank."

"Yeah, I know. Anyway, I went down there after school, while you guys were at soccer. I wanted to check it out and ... okay, you guys are not going to believe this—"

"Tell us!" yelled Morgan.

"There's more than thirty thousand dollars in there!"

"No way!" screamed Emily.

"That's a whole lotta money!" yelled Carlie.

"Wowzers!" exclaimed Morgan.

"It's like a real miracle," said Chelsea in a stunned voice.

"Yeah, that's what I thought too," said Amy.

"Who donated that much money?" asked Morgan.

"A number of people," said Amy. "They have a list, but there is also one anonymous donor, someone who gave most of the money."

"Who do you think it was?" asked Emily.

"Well, it's hard to believe this, but I think maybe it was Viola McPhearson."

"Really?" Morgan didn't look convinced.

"I know, it sounds strange, but I have a feeling ..."

"Well, that's not important now," said Morgan. "What's important now is figuring out how we can make this happen before the thirty-day deadline."

"That's right," said Amy. "I've already done a little research, made some phone calls, and I already have a few things lined up for tomorrow." She pulled out her list and the names and numbers. "I've tried to make a budget," she said. "And after talking to several people, I can see how thirty thousand dollars may sound like a lot, but it's going to be tight."

The girls studied the list and made some comments and suggestions. Then they split up some of the phone numbers and tasks, and everyone went to work making phone calls and lining things up for tomorrow.

On Saturday morning all five girls met at the park at the crack of dawn. And before long the first dump truck filled with bark mulch arrived. Shortly after that, a load of grass turf arrived. But the most amazing thing to arrive was *people*! Dressed for work and equipped with rakes and shovels, lots of people showed up and got very busy. There were neighbors from Harbor View Mobile-Home Court — even Mr. Greeley, who usually kept to himself, had come!

"Did you see the article in this morning's paper?" Gary asked Amy as he dumped a load of beach sand in the play area where she was spreading it.

"No," she told him. "I never had time to look at the paper."

He pulled a folded page out of his sweatshirt pocket and opened it up. There on the front page were Amy and her friends, looking dirty but happy. And then there was another shot of the park sign where they had planted the shrubs and trees from the woods. The headline said, "Park Preservationists Refuse to Give Up." She scanned the article then smiled. "Thanks, Mr. Hardwick."

"Thank *you*, Amy." He grinned at her. "You and your friends had the right idea from the start. It's just too bad it took everyone else so long to figure it out."

"But at least they figured it out," she said, looking out over the park, which was looking more and more like a park.

By the end of the day, it really did look like a miracle had hit McPhearson Park. With the combined efforts of the volunteers, hired workers, and contractors, everything was back into place — only now it was much better than before.

"This is truly amazing," said the mayor as he surveyed the freshly laid turf with new park benches along the edges. He had actually been working with them for the better part of the day. "I never would've believed this was possible."

"That's what makes it a miracle," said Amy.

"This park used to be a real eyesore," said Gary Hardwick as he took another photo of a completed section of the project. "And now it's really beautiful."

Two weeks later, the city sponsored a ceremony to celebrate the park's renovation, which was finally complete.

But when the girls arrived early on Saturday afternoon, they were shocked to see a large construction truck with a big yellow crane just pulling out onto the street.

"What's up with that?" asked Amy with concern. "Don't tell me they are putting in a parking lot after all."

"No way," said Carlie. "They wouldn't dare."

"Although we did miss the thirty-day deadline," Amy pointed out.

They all ran over to see what was going on. They all stopped in their tracks when they saw something that hadn't been there before. In the center of the park, looking as if it had always been there, sat a big white gazebo.

"It's beautiful!" exclaimed Carlie.

"Wow!" yelled Emily.

"Miss McPhearson," said Amy.

"She did this?" asked Morgan.

"I'm sure she did," said Amy. "There used to be a gazebo here when she was a girl. Mrs. Watson said they had concerts in the park."

"Cool," said Chelsea.

Soon all the chairs and things were arranged for the ceremony, situated all around the gazebo. The five girls were invited to sit up front with the mayor. Just as the mayor stood up, preparing to give a dedication speech, Amy noticed an elderly woman slowly making her way across the park.

"It's Miss McPhearson," she whispered to the mayor.

"I thought you said she wasn't coming," said the mayor.

Amy grinned. "That's what she told me several times, but then Miss McPhearson is a little unpredictable." Then Amy left the gazebo and ran down to meet the old woman. Taking her hand, Amy led her up to the gazebo where she was given the seat of honor, right in the center.

"I'm so glad you came," whispered Amy.

"Harrumph."

The mayor made a nice speech about how important it was to preserve old traditions and historical places, and he was just finishing up when Miss McPhearson stood and cleared her throat.

"Would you like to share a few words?" he asked her, looking a bit uncomfortable.

"Yes." She stepped up to the microphone. "As many of you know, my family founded this park many, many years ago. And for generations it was a good place for people to gather, for children to play ... but it fell into disrepair and many felt it should be tossed aside, the way people do with old things." She sighed. "But these five young ladies saw beyond the oldness. Or, as my friend Amy Ngo would say, they weren't afraid to dream. I think we can all learn a lot from them. But I'm not here to go on and on. I am here to say that I am donating this park to the city, but with the condition that it will always remain a park. And I will also donate a trust fund to help with the maintenance." She stepped aside now and everyone clapped.

Miss McPhearson sat back down next to Amy and turned to her. "But I do have one condition, Amy Ngo."

"What?"

"You and your friends must come to tea again." She almost smiled now. "We have much to talk about."

"It's a deal," said Amy, sticking out her hand to shake with Miss McPhearson.

Amy looked out over the spectators sitting in the folding chairs in their recently renovated city park. She could see her family sitting near the back. Even her mother was there. And to Amy's surprise, she too was smiling.

Amy whispered a silent prayer. She thanked God for working miracles — and she thanked him for planting new dreams in her heart.

Girls of Harbor View
by Melody Carlson!

Harbor view was no place for a girl ... until now. Meet Morgan, Amy, Carlie, and Emily, unlikely friends brought together when they come to live in the Harbor View Trailer Park. Discover what happens when they join forces to make their world a better place.

Girl Power

Take Charge

Raising Faith

Secret Admirer

Available in stores and online!